Unraveling You
a Novel

By Jessica Sorensen

For information:

jessicasorensen.com

Cover Design by Okay Creations

Photography: Perrywinkle Photography

Unraveling You (Unraveling, #1)

ISBN: 978-1496134271

Chapter 1

Lyric

16 years old…

The couple that lives next door adopts children like puppies. No joke. The Gregorys are bringing home kid number four today. The adoption process has happened so frequently over the years for them that it's become a routine. They drive off in the early morning, cruising away in their sedan, and then late in the afternoon they return with a small human being sitting in the backseat, looking about as scared as a little puppy getting yelled at.

While I do feel sorry for the little boy or girl, the sympathy quickly wears off. Because within a couple of months, the small human in the backseat will get over their fear and turn into their own person, who more than likely will take it upon themselves to annoy the crap out of me.

I'd be fine with this. After all, they are my next-door neighbors' kids, not my little brothers or sisters. But that's the thing. They *are* kind of like the little brother or sister I never had, since the couple next door are my parents' best friends and close to a second set of parents to me. I even call them Aunt Lila and Uncle Ethan.

"I wonder what this one will look like," I remark as I munch on my toast at the kitchen table. It's late morning, but we're late risers, so we're just starting breakfast, even though it's past ten. "And if it'll be a boy or a girl."

"Lila said he was a boy," my mother answers as she collects her mug and takes a seat across from me. "I think he's about your age, too."

"All their adopted kids are older. Aren't people supposed to adopt younger children?" I ask, reaching for the butter. "Like when they're babies?"

She sips the coffee then places the mug on the table. "Lyric, there are a ton of kids out there that need homes, both young and your age. Even older. You should realize just how lucky you are to have a roof over your head and parents who spoil the crap out of you. Some children don't have it so lucky."

My mother is probably one of the strangest moms ever, but in the best way possible. She uses phrases like, "spoil the crap out of you," and dresses cooler than I do half the time. Plus, she has fantastic taste in music.

"I know how lucky I am," I tell her. "So lucky in fact, that I know you're going to let me paint my room purple and black."

"Let me guess. Purple walls and black skulls."

"Hey, how'd you guess?"

"Because it's exactly how my room looked when I was your age. You're so much like me it's frightening sometimes."

"Well, there goes my theory that I was secretly adopted."

I don't really have that theory. I resemble my parents too much to ever believe I was adopted. I have my mother's striking green eyes, so bright they sometimes startle people at first glance. And I have the same shade of blonde hair my dad does. They're both tall, too, and passed that trait to me. At sixteen, I round in at five foot nine and tower over all of my friends at school. I inherited some of their talents as well, that is, if talents can be inherited.

Like my mother, I have the hand of an artist, although she is way better than I am. She owns her own art gallery and has sold a lot of her paintings. Her work is usually described as raw, emotional, and realistic.

Then there's my dad's talent of music. My father is a musician who used to perform in a band, and then later on as a solo artist. Now, he's mostly retired and owns his own studio. I'm not sure if it was all the time I spent hanging out with him, or the fact that my parents named me Lyric, but music is branded into my bones. I love anything and everything that has to do with it. My favorite instrument is the guitar, granted the violin is a close second. Creating lyrics, though, that's truly my favorite thing to do musically.

"It seems like such a nice day to go out for a drive," my mother comments, bringing me out of my thoughts and back to reality. "Maybe when Lila gets home, the three of us and the new boy can go for a drive. It'll give you some time to get to know him."

I stuff the rest of my toast into my mouth. "What if he's weird, though, like Kale?"

Kale is the latest addition to the Gregory family. He was twelve when they brought him home two years ago, and he still hasn't given up his obsession with comic books. And I mean *obsession*. He frequently dresses up like characters, his favorite being Flash. He also once wore a cape to school, which made him the subject of a lot of bullying.

Then there are the other two kiddos, Fiona and Ever-

8

son. At twelve, Fiona is the youngest and probably the chattiest. She loves to draw and has a deep fascination with butterflies. Everson is smack dab between Fiona and Kale at thirteen years old. He's quiet, loves sports, especially football, and is probably the most normal of the bunch. They all have their weird little quirks, though, and shady pasts that I never really get to fully hear.

It's not like I have anything against weirdoes and shady pasts—heck, I can be a weirdo and sketchy sometimes—but as the sorta bigger sister, I constantly have to stick up for them, and sometimes it gets tiring.

"Lyric, just because Kale's different doesn't mean he's weird." My mom reaches for the coffee pot. "Need I remind you of your little obsession with that boy band when you were his age."

"You promised you'd never bring that up. You even pinkie swore that you wouldn't."

Her lips curl as she fills her cup to the brim with steaming hot coffee. "Then don't give me reasons to break my promise."

"Fine, I'll stop calling Kale a weirdo on one condition." I swallow a gulp of milk then wipe my lips with the back of my hand. "If you let me go to the concert on Friday with Dad."

Her cheeriness diminishes. "Did he tell you that you could go with him?"

I shrug. "He didn't not tell me I couldn't."

She shakes her head, restraining a grin. "You are way too good of a bargainer for your own good."

I perk up. "So does that mean I can go?"

"Hmm ... That all depends on if you'll go on a drive with me later and warmly welcome the new Gregory." She raises her glass to her mouth, but only to hide a smirk.

"Touché, Mother. I see where I get my bargaining skills from."

I consider her offer. Going on a drive with my mother may not seem like the most fun thing in the world, but it kind of is. Her and my dad used to drag race, and they still have some of their badass cars we take out when we go for trips. Both of them drive fast, although I think they play it safe when I'm in the car. It's still fun, though.

What makes me hesitate on the offer is the getting to know the new Gregory part. Like puppies, I never know what the new addition's personality is going to be. He could be nice, or he could be a little weirdo who bites. The youngest, Fiona, actually bit me the first day they brought her home.

But I want to go to the concert badly enough that the pros outweigh the cons.

I chug the rest of my milk then agree. "Fine, I'll go with you as long as you let me go with Dad."

"Go where with me?" my dad asks as he strolls into the kitchen carrying his guitar case.

I scoot back from the table and stand up. "To the concert."

My dad drops his guitar case to the floor and lifts his hand for a high five. "See, I told you it'd be better if you asked her."

My mother's head whips in his direction, and she scowls at him. "Did you put her up to that?"

He shrugs as I slam my palm against his. "You have a hard time telling her no."

"So do you." She narrows her eyes. "You spoil her too much."

"And vice versa." He leans down and whispers something in her ear, causing her to giggle and blush.

That is my cue to leave, because in just a few moments, they'll start making out like they always do. *So gross.*

I hurry out of the kitchen and up to my bedroom to change out of my pajamas. I select a black tank top and a pair of cut offs then braid my long, blonde hair before applying a dab of eyeliner around my eyes. I then blast some Rise Against and rock out on my drums for a bit. Uncle Ethan actually taught me how to play, but he says I'm a natural since I caught on really quick.

After the drums comes the guitar. I turn on "Buried Myself Alive" by The Used and strum the strings to the tempo until my fingers are numb. Then I crank up some "Lithium" by Evanescence and go mad crazy with the violin while belting out the lyrics. I stop when I'm hoarse and flop down on my bed to draw covers for the albums I have yet to create.

Once my hands ache, I move on to lyrics. Although it's one of my favorite things to do, I sometimes feel like I lack in the lyrical department. Most of the music I love is angsty, emotional, semi-twisted, and moves the soul. Mine always seem to come out on the exuberant side. I'm hoping with time it will change. I know my dad wrote some of his best lyrics in his late teen years, when he was pining over my mom. He even told me once that the more I experience life, the more emotional my songs will get. Now, if I could just get those experiences like he said, life would be fantastic.

I'm still figuring out how to attain that life, though. For the most part, my life is pretty boring. I have decent, pretty cool parents who support every dream I throw at them, whether it's proclaiming that I'm going to create my own genre in music, or win a Grammy. I get to do a lot of things I want to do, like go to concerts, art shows, meet semi-famous musicians. I've spent a lot of time in my dad's studio, watching artists record. I have a lot of friends, granted none of them I would consider a best friend, but there are still occasions where I feel lonely.

Bored. Ordinary. That's what my life is. And ordinary doesn't make awesome music.

Plus, even if I miraculously became the most killer songwriter ever, I could never sing in front of anyone. Just playing the guitar for my family makes me want to vomit. Singing is much more raw than playing an instrument. Much more real. Exposes the soul so much more. And as blunt as I am, exposing my soul freaks the living shit out of

Jessica Sorensen

me, because I fear people won't like what's in me.

By the time I look up from the notepad again, the sun is setting over the city of San Diego, and the sky is shades of florescent pink and orange.

"Lyric, it's time!" my mother calls up the stairs as I'm tucking my notepad under my pillow.

Sighing, I slip on my black boots and trot down the stairs.

"How long of a drive does it have to be?" I ask her as I wander into the living room where she's stacking our entire DVD collection onto the coffee table.

Movie watching is an adoption day tradition. We start off with dinner at the Gregory's, where everyone gets reacquainted with each other. Then we come over here to watch a movie since we have a massive television in our living room.

"I'm not sure yet." She stands up straight and gathers lose strands of her red hair out of her face while she scans the room. She has spots of grey and blue paint in her hair and on her cheek, which means she's been in her studio for most of the day. "I feel like I'm forgetting something."

"Batteries. You've been meaning to change them for like two weeks." I chuck her the remote that I collect from

14

the armrest.

She catches it. "Yeah, that's it. What would I do without you?"

"Probably lose your marbles."

She pats my head as she rushes out of the living room. Minutes later, she returns with the remote and my dad in tow.

"Everyone ready?" she asks as she tosses the remote onto the sofa. "Let's go."

"Do I really have to go this time?" I whisper to my dad as we follow my mom out the door and into the dwindling sunlight. "It's starting to get really old. I mean, I'll get to see the newbie tomorrow. And the day after that. And the day after that."

My dad swings an arm around me as we step off the front porch. "Lyric, I know you don't get it now, but one day you'll see the importance."

I look up at him. "In what?"

"In the family you have," he says as we round the picket fence on the line of our property. We hike up the Gregory's driveway to their two-story home that is very similar to ours. The only noticeable difference on the outside is the shade of the siding—white and grey. "You're really lucky to have *every* single one of us. And you should really get to know the new kid. He's your age, and I'm sure he could use a friend with … some of the stuff he's been through. You could be that friend for him. Do something good."

I wonder what he means by *stuff*.

"I know I'm lucky, and I was planning on getting to know him." *Sort of.* "And I do good stuff all the time. I go with Mom and Lila to the shelter every year on Thanksgiving and help out. I give my clothes away sometimes. I even befriended Maggie McMellford last year, despite the fact that no one was nice to her and she didn't know who Nirvana was until I let her listen to them."

"Really? She didn't know who Nirvana was?"

I shrug. "Unfortunately, a lot of kids don't have an old man musician father who knows all the classics."

"Old man?" His brow arches. "Ha, ha, you're a riot, Lyric Scott."

I innocently grin at him. "I wasn't trying to be a riot. Just telling the truth."

He chuckles and I laugh with him. My laughter silences, though, as the Gregory's enormous sedan rolls up the drive.

I sigh as my gaze instantly drifts to the backseat, searching for the scared little puppy dog. All I find is what appears to be a guy crammed in with the rest of the Gregory clan. I'm not one-hundred percent sure what he looks like, since I don't have a clear view into the backseat, so I wait in anticipation until the sedan parks and the clan piles out.

Normally, the newbie remains in the backseat, too afraid to leave the vehicle. This one just hops right out and rounds the car toward us as if he doesn't have a care in the world.

He doesn't look like the rest of them either. Honestly, he kind of looks like Uncle Ethan in the pictures I've seen of him when he was younger. Black hair, dark eyes, tall. He's dressed head-to-toe in black, wearing a … I squint to see if I'm seeing things correctly. Yep, he's wearing a leather collar around his neck.

I'm not sure what to make of this. What it says about him. At my school, the kids who dress like this are the rebellious troublemakers. Is that how he's going to be? Part of me is thrilled at the idea, while the other fears it.

"Everyone, this is Ayden," Aunt Lila introduces him with the proudest smile as she gently places her hand on Ayden's shoulder.

Ayden glances at her hand, and by the hardness in his eyes, I expect him to get angry with her, but he doesn't utter a word.

"And, Ayden, these are our neighbors, Micha and Ella Scott." Lila motions her hand at me. "And this is their daughter, Lyric."

Smiling, I wave. "Hi."

He doesn't say hi back. Doesn't wave either. He just stares at me. And stares. He stares so long that I get a bit uncomfortable, especially because of the sadness radiating from his eyes. It's kind of hard to endure and makes me feel subdued. I consider ducking behind my dad to escape his stare down, but I'm guessing I'd get scolded for being rude so I keep my feet planted and focus on my fingernails, picking at the black nail polish.

I listen to everyone yammer, squirming more and more the longer Ayden's sad eyes remain fastened on me, as if he's daring me to figure out all of his secrets, his weirdo side, his shady past.

Finally, we all file inside the house and I breathe freely

again as he stops focusing on me and instead zeros in on his new home.

Lila starts giving him a tour of the house while Ethan leads the other three rugrats into the kitchen with my dad.

I start to go with my dad, but my mom captures me by the back of my shirt and tows me back to her. "Let's go with them." She nods at Lila and Ayden as they ascend the stairway.

I scrunch up my nose as I recollect Ayden's intense, depressing stare. "Do I have to? He looks so sad, and his staring is making me uncomfortable."

"All the more reason to spend time with him." She signals for me to get a move on. I reluctantly obey, but stand as far behind as I can without looking too antisocial.

Luckily, Ayden seems more engrossed with the home and his room than me. He doesn't even glance my way as he takes in each wall, piece of furniture, and framed pictures. But when we all gather around the table for dinner, he ends up sitting across from me, and the stare down begins again.

I attempt to avoid his gaze as he watches me pick at my salad. As I chow down on my burger. As I chat with

Fiona about her art obsession. The longer the staring goes on, the squirrelier I become, until I can't take it anymore.

Throwing my napkin onto the table, I slump back in the chair, cross my arms, and stare at him in the same manner.

At first, he appears unfazed, but as the minutes tick by, he starts to look almost amused.

Interesting.

Without removing his eyes from me, he picks up his drink and guzzles a long swallow. I do the same. We simultaneously place our glasses down. He pauses then drums his fingers on the table, either testing me or playing with me ... I'm still not sure yet.

Intrigued, I thrum my fingers, too.

He fiddles with the small black and red gauge in his left ear. I only have one piercing in each of mine and no earrings in right now, but I still pretend to mess around with an invisible gauge.

He rolls his tongue across his teeth, the smallest trace of a ghost smile emerging. I feel like I've won a game and delve forward, determined to make that sadness crack.

"Oh, Lyric, let me play, too!" Fiona clasps her hands together as she kneels up on her chair. "Pretty please. I've never had a brother to play copycat with before. Kale and Everson always get so angry."

I smirk at Ayden then turn to her. "I think Ayden would love to play with you." I rise from the table, take my dirty dishes to the sink, and sneak outside to get some fresh air.

As I'm sitting on the curb in front of the house with my legs stretched out, I catch Ayden gawking at me through his upstairs bedroom window. I tip my head to the side, wondering just how long this whole staring thing is going to last. He hasn't even spoken a word yet.

Maybe he doesn't speak.

"Lyric!" my mother suddenly shouts, and I tear my attention away from the window. She's exiting the house with Lila, both of them elated about something. "Ready to go out on a drive with us?"

"Surely durely." I stand up and brush the dirt off the backs of my legs then start to follow them to my house when Lila glances back at me.

"Lyric, would you mind running up and telling Ayden to come with us?" she asks, hopeful. "He seems a little nervous except when he's around you."

My brows furrow. "He hasn't even said a word to me, so how do you arrive at that conclusion?"

"Well, you two were playing that little staring contest game at the table." She adjusts the pale pink strap of her purse higher on her shoulder. "I would really appreciate it, sweetie."

My Aunt Lila is way too nice to argue with, so I reel around to go get Ayden, but then halt before I reach the front steps.

"Aunt Lila, does Ayden ... talk?" I dare ask, facing her again.

"Of course, sweetie. He's just a little nervous. Things have been hard for him, and I think he's feeling a little overwhelmed."

She turns to my mom and starts telling her about the countless foster families he grew up in and that he has some problems.

"He's been through so much," she says with a disheartened sigh, pressing her hand to her chest. "And still has so much to face in the future."

I stop to listen, but when my mom shoots me a death glare, I hurry into the house and up the stairs to Ayden's bedroom.

His door is wide open and he's sitting on the edge of the bed, staring at a duffel bag on the floor. He looks so morose that I feel kind of sorry for him. *What has this boy been through?*

"You're supposed to come downstairs and go on a drive," I announce as I waltz into the room.

He jumps, startled as his attention darts up to me. He doesn't reply. Simply just stares again.

"I know it sounds really lame." I wander around, observing all the knickknacks Lila put up—sports and band posters, little painted blocks with quotes on them, books on the shelf. It's like she didn't know what he was into, so she just decorated the room with a bit of everything. "It's pretty fun, though. They drive fast and stuff."

He still doesn't utter a word. Just looks at me.

I face the bed and assess him while he studies me back. His head is tilted just enough that his black hair dangles in his grey eyes, so I don't have a clear view of how he's looking at me. He appears uneasy, though, fidgeting with a bracelet on his wrist.

Finally, I can't take the silence anymore. Even though I know I might get in trouble for doing it, if he chooses to

23

tell on me, I march to the bed and stand right in front of him.

When he angles his head back to look at me, his eyes are filled with confusion. I poke him in the side of the ribs, hard enough that he flinches and his body jolts.

"What the hell?" He gapes at me as he cradles his side.

"Ha!" I cry, pointing a finger at him. "You do know how to speak."

His lips part in astonishment. "Of course I know how to speak."

"No, of course you know how to stare. Speaking was getting a little questionable. Either you couldn't speak or you were just shy, but I needed to find out."

He has no clue how to respond to my colorful personality—most people don't in the beginning.

Feeling a little on the adventurous side, I snatch ahold of Ayden's hand and drag him to his feet. "Come on, shy boy." I pull him with me as I march out of the room and downstairs. "The longer we stay up here, the longer this night is going to drag on."

He follows me a lot easier than I expected him to, holding onto my hand, maybe too tightly, as if he's terrified out of his wits.

"I thought you said driving with them was fun?" he questions. "So why would you want the night to end so soon?"

"The driving part is fun," I assure him as I throw open the front door. The cool breeze kisses my skin and it smells like leaves and grass. "But the movie thing at the end is painful to endure. We always have to watch a kid appropriate movie. Either a cartoon or something rated PG." I glance back at him. "Although, maybe because you're older, they'll let us watch something cooler."

"Maybe I like cartoons and PG movies," he counters, holding my gaze as he slides his hand from mine and folds his arms across his chest.

"Do you?"

"Not really. I just wanted to make a point. You shouldn't make assumptions. Maybe I'm a kid at heart who likes kid movies."

"You know what, Ayden? I think you and I might be good friends, if you're lucky." I snatch his hand again and tug him around the fence and up the driveway toward the open garage of my house. "Although, you still have to pass the music quiz."

"Music quiz?" he asks, distracted by my mother's black and red 1969 GTO parked in the garage next to my dad's 1969 Chevelle SS, staring at both of them in awe, like most guys do.

"Yeah. Music. As in instruments and lyrics and stuff. I might not be able to be friends with you if you like some of that cliché pop music they always play on the radio."

He cocks a brow at me. "Do I look like someone who's into that kind of music?"

I release his hand as we near the car then smirk at him. "Well, my initial assumption would be a no, but you told me not to make assumptions."

"But I didn't expect you to listen."

I wink at him. "I'm an excellent listener, along with many other awesome things." I skip around to the driver's side and dive into the backseat, giving the horn a couple of honks on my way.

"Get in!" I call out to Ayden as I push the passenger door open for him.

A second later, he slides onto the leather seat beside me.

"Where are they?" he asks as he settles in the seat, fidgeting with the leather band on his wrist.

"Who knows?" I lean over the console and pound on the horn until the door to the house swings open.

My mom and Lila come wandering out, scolding me for the horn honks. Their scolding is nothing new. I easily shrug it off and sit back in the seat as the drive begins.

My mother does her best not to peel the tires until we're on the freeway, since the last time she did it out of the driveway the neighbors made a complaint. Once we're on the long, curvy stretch of road, though, all bets are off.

"Just take it a bit easy, Ella," Lila begs as she clutches the seat, something she always does when we go driving. "We have a newbie to your … um, interesting driving skills."

"Awesome driving skills." My mother smiles at me from the rearview mirror and I grin back, knowing what's coming.

An instant later, she punches the gas and we're off, flying down the road and weaving in and out of cars.

I relax and breathe in the air blowing through the window. Out of the corner of my eye, I catch Ayden picking at his black fingernail polish.

I stick out my hand and wiggle my fingers. "Look. We

match."

Again, he nearly smiles, but I've still yet to witness any sort of happiness from him. It's got me curious, way more curious than the other kids Aunt Lila and Uncle Ethan have brought home. They all have their sad moments, but not like this, so sullen all the time. It makes me want to get him to smile really, really badly.

"Hey, Mom," I say, without taking my eyes off Ayden. "Can we turn on some music?"

"Sure. What do you want to listen to?"

"Can I just see your iPod?"

She hands it to me, and I give it to Ayden. "Here you go." I slip off my sandals and kick my feet up on the console. "Impress me."

I wait patiently as his eyes dance between me and the iPod in his hand. He starts sorting through the songs. I swear he just about grins again when he makes his selection and returns the device back to me. I pause as I take it from him, catching a glimpse of a row of thin scars that look like cat scratches on the top of his hand. Noticing the direction of my gaze, he quickly jerks his sleeve over his hand then rotates toward the window again.

I want to ask him about the scars. I want to ask him a

lot of things. But I force my curious side to shut up and focus on the music. The song he chose causes me to laugh,
because of all things it's by Nirvana. I start singing along
under my breath, quiet enough that no one can actually hear
me, while Ayden thrums his fingers to the beat, gazing out
the window at the houses and stores in the distance.

"Are you sure you're not too hot?" Lila asks Ayden for
the millionth time, making her seem way more doting toward him than she was with the other three.

"I'm good," he responds, scratching at the scars on the
back of his hand as he turns inward.

"You know what would be cool," I say when the silence gets to me. "If Ayden could come to the concert with
Dad and me."

"Oh, he can't." Lila fretfully glances over her shoulder
at Ayden, who doesn't say a thing. "Ayden has to take it
easy for the first few weeks while he's here, getting adjust-
ed to everything. I don't want to over-excite him."

So strange.

I sit back in the seat as we continue to drive through
the city for the next hour before returning home. As we hop
out of the car to go inside the house and watch a movie, I

snag Ayden's sleeve and draw him back to me. When Lila and my mom step inside, I release his shirt and face him.

"Okay, you passed the music test. Now we can be friends." I would have been friends with him anyway, but it's more entertaining this way.

He stares me down. "What if I don't want to be friends with you?"

I'm unsure if he's being serious or not, but I shrug him off, seeing this as more of a fun challenge than anything else.

"You do. I promise. Not only am I the most awesome person ever, but I can show you the ropes of your new life." I stick out my hand. "So what do you say? Friends?"

He eyeballs my hand then his gaze glides up my body and lands on my face. "All right, we can be friends, Lyric." He places his scarred hand in mine and we shake on it.

His fingers tremor as we pull away, and his smile never fully reaches his eyes.

I know the story. All of the children Lila and Ethan have adopted have been through something terrible. Usually, I leave it alone since it's none of my business, but with Ayden, I'm curious. I have questions. Lots and lots of questions.

I make a vow to myself right then and there that one day, as his friend, I will get to know him and find out his story.

Then, I'll make him smile for real.

Chapter 2

Ayden

Just breathe. Just breathe. Just Breathe.
The pressure will crack and shatter
if you just keep breathing.
Life will eventually get easier
if you keep your heart beating.
Just breathe. Just breathe. Just breathe.

I repeat the mantra of words over in my mind the entire drive to my new house, all during the tour, and during the ride with the woman who drives crazier than most teenagers. I chant it under my breath all night long when I don't get an ounce of sleep.

The process is nothing new. This is the sixth time I've lay awake in a new room within the last year. Stability is what's uncertain to me, even before I entered the system. And now, suddenly, they're telling me I have it. That this home is *the* home. That I'm being adopted and will no longer be passed around from family to family.

I don't understand it. Teenagers aren't supposed to be

adopted. No one wants them, especially ones that are as ruined as I am, that have been through the things I have. We're stray dogs, scraggily, ratty, bad habits, untrainable. People want puppies. Cute, fixable puppies. Yet here I am, supposedly wanted by the Gregorys, despite my scars and issues.

The house is strangely quiet at night, and even during the brink of morning. Maybe I'm just too used to a lot of noise, but the soundlessness makes sleep impossible. I end up staring at the ceiling until the sun peeks over the city and heats up the room. Then I climb out of bed and start to get ready for school.

After I pull on a pair of faded black jeans and a matching shirt, I sit on the bed and stare at the few contents inside my bag. A single photo of me with my older brother and younger sister, a rusty pocketknife, and a watch are all that's left of my original life—the one that I was born into. I don't miss that life at all, but I miss my brother and sister, who I haven't seen since social services barged in on that God awful day and yanked us out of that shithole house.

I look down at the scars on the backs of my hands. Marks of my past, branded forever into my body and soul. I can remember clearly how some of them were put onto my body. Others I can't. The freshest ones are the worst. They happened the day I was taken away, a day my mind has somehow blocked.

They'll never go away.

Always own a fragment of my soul.

Own a part of me.

Never let me go.

Yet they won't own the pieces

that live in the darkest parts.

There, but not quite breathing.

Please, please don't let them break me apart.

I put the photo down and pick up the other object hidden beneath the small pile of clothes—a bottle of pills I stole from the last home. I don't even know why I took it. Not to get high. I'm not into drugs. I just wanted to have them, just in case I can't take this anymore, the pain and darkness and ugliness residing inside me. The loneliness. The unknown.

I wonder if I should take them now. All of them. Then I wouldn't have to face another damn day feeling as though the ground is about to crack apart beneath me. Face the world being friendless again. Alone. Always alone. I hate it, but can't admit it aloud.

"Ayden."

Mrs. Gregory is standing in the doorway with her blonde hair pulled up, wearing a hesitant expression. She has on a red apron over jeans and a long-sleeved shirt. She looks like a typical mom, yet her warming, comforting demeanor is unfamiliar to me.

"I was coming to wake you up for school"—she tentatively steps foot into the room, glancing around at everything still neatly in place like it was yesterday. I haven't dared touch anything except the bed—"but it looks like you're already ready."

I nod as I drop the bottle into the duffel bag and quickly fasten the zipper. Her eyes track my movements, and I half expect her to ask me what I'm doing, but she doesn't.

"Do you want some breakfast?" She points over her shoulder at the doorway. "I made chocolate chip pancakes."

I rake my hand through my shaggy black hair as I spring to my feet and fumble for my tattered backpack on the floor. "Sure, ma'am."

She frowns. "Ayden, you don't need to call me ma'am."

I seal my lips together and remain silent. I've never been much of a talker, nor do I feel comfortable calling her anything but ma'am. Yes, they're officially adopting me now, but we'll see how long that lasts. I give them a week until they want to send me back.

She stiffly smiles then signals for me to follow her as she starts for the door. "Come on. Let's get some breakfast in you while Kale's getting ready. I'll have Ethan drive you all to school. He takes the rest of the kids a little bit later since junior high starts later than the high school."

I nod, slinging the handle of my bag over my shoulder. "Okay."

She seems unnerved by my one-word responses, but I don't know how to give her more.

She pauses when we reach the arch of the kitchen doorway. "Are you sure you're up for school? Because you could always skip a few days and start next week when you're a little bit used to things. And I could take you shopping for some new clothes."

I shake my head. "I'm fine. I'm used to stuff already. And I'm fine with my clothes."

She offers me a sad smile. "If that's what you want."

I freeze, thrown off balance. I'm pretty certain that's

the first time someone has said something like that to me. "Yeah, that's ... what I want."

She whisks into the kitchen, crossing the length of the large room and heading toward the stainless steel stove. The entire house is big and sparkly—fancy. I feel very uncomfortable, because all the other homes I've been in have been small, dull, and broken.

"I'll see if Lyric wants to ride with you," she says as she refastens the tie on her apron. "She's a junior like you. It might be nice to know someone your age."

The suggestion makes me uneasy. Lyric made me feel out of my element yesterday with her blunt, bold attitude. Plus, her green eyes are so unbelievably intense that I had trouble looking away from them. I think I came off even more insane than I normally do. Still, after all the staring, the damn girl seemed determined to be my friend. I haven't had much in the line of friends, and wouldn't even know what to do with one, but I still agreed to be hers, figuring I'd only be here for a week, so keeping my promise wouldn't matter.

"Are you okay with that?" Mrs. Gregory begins stirring batter in a bowl.

Jessica Sorensen

I nod as I take a seat at the rectangular table in the nook. "Yeah, that's fine."

I can tell she's about to explode from my limited answers. I wait for her to yell at me—it wouldn't be the first time I've been yelled at by an adult for my silence. Instead, she offers me pancakes, so many that I feel fuller than I ever have, as if she whole-heartedly believes that pancakes are the way to cure my silence.

I wish they were.

Chocolate chips to heal a broken soul.

Cure hunger.

Cure the past.

Cure my amnesia.

Lyric had warned me yesterday, though, that Mrs. Gregory would be like this. That she runs her own catering business on the weekends and loves to do experimental cooking for the family whenever she can.

After I assure Mrs. Gregory that I'm stuffed, she ushers Mr. Gregory, Kale, and I out the door, shoving a granola bar and banana in Kale's hand.

"Oh, and remember you have therapy later today," Mrs. Gregory subtly reminds me on my way out.

I nod, even though I'm not a fan of the idea, and follow Kale and Mr. Gregory out the door. We get into a bulky black sedan that seems more like a chauffeur car than a family vehicle. Then, Mr. Gregory backs down the driveway, pausing at the street where he lays on the horn, staring at the neighbors' house.

"You should get along with Lyric just fine. She's a very outgoing girl." That's all he says. He was the same way yesterday. A man of few words. I think I might kind of like him.

I fasten my seatbelt while we all wait in silence. A couple of minutes later, a very bouncy Lyric comes bounding out of the house with her backpack on. The girl walks like she's on crack, all bouncy and full of sunshine. I find myself both envious and mesmerized by it—by her.

Her long blonde hair is down and blowing in the breeze. She's wearing red cut-offs with a long-sleeved black shirt that has netting for the sleeves. I'm still trying to figure out what kind of person she is. At first glance, I might have gone with Goth—minus the blond hair—but after watching her smile and chat yesterday, she seems too cheery for that type of crowd. Cheerleader doesn't seem right either. Neither does a jock.

"Hello, everyone," Lyric singsongs as she hoists herself into the backseat of the sedan and scoots in next to Kale. She has a violin case in one hand and a Pop Tart in the other.

Orchestra freak? Wouldn't have guessed that.

"Morning, Lyric," Mr. Gregory replies as she slams the car door. He backs out onto the road and drives down the street, past the two-story homes, and toward the stop sign. "What's your dad up to today?"

Lyric briefly flashes Kale a smile, who goes as stiff as a board, then she buckles her seatbelt and peers up front at me.

I realize I'm staring again. I tell myself to look away, but like yesterday, I'm too curious to listen to myself.

"Not much," she tells Mr. Gregory as she munches on her breakfast. "I think he's going to go down to his studio and rock out for a little while. Why? You thinking about having an old man jam session?"

Mr. Gregory shakes his head, but I can tell he's trying really hard not to smile. "I'm not that old, Lyric."

She pats him on the shoulder. "It's okay. I won't tell anyone."

He rolls his eyes. "So, how are the drums coming

along?"

She shrugs as she unzips her backpack. "Good. Although I still think I'm way better at the guitar and violin. The drums are fun, though, for letting some steam off."

So she plays the guitar, drums, and violin. Okay, she's not an orchestra freak, just a hardcore music freak. It makes me like her more.

While I don't know how to play any instrument, listening to music is a huge outlet for me and got me through a lot of hard times. Plus, it drowns out screaming really well.

"And how about the lyric writing?" he asks as he veers the sedan onto the main road that centers the small, upper class neighborhood.

She retrieves a pack of gum then sets the bag aside. "Not that great, but I blame it on my parents. They've made my life too easy, and I have absolutely nothing to write about."

"You could always write about the easy stuff," he suggests, looking at me for some reason, as if he knows my not-so-easy secrets.

She pops a piece of gum into her mouth then offers one to Kale, who quickly shakes his head. "I don't want to be that kind of a songwriter."

Mr. Gregory glances at her through the rearview mirror. "You sound just like your dad."

"Thanks." She seems proud of this, something I find strange. Most kids my age would take it as an insult.

Her eyes abruptly lock on mine. "Do you play anything, shy boy?"

Great. She's already given me a nickname.

I shake my head. "No."

"What do you do, then?"

I shrug. "Nothing."

She leans forward in the seat, chomping on her gum. "Now, that's not true. I mean, clearly you've got a chance for the Most-One-Word-Responses championship title." She blows a bubble, and then smiles at me, making happiness look so effortless.

"Well, obviously there's that," I retort, unable to help myself. "But I'm betting my chances for winning are going to go down the more time I spend with you."

She grins as she reclines back into the seat. "Excellent comeback, shy boy."

I'm on the verge of smiling as I face forward in the seat again, but any trace of happiness dissipates when we pull up to the school. It was clear to me yesterday, when I first saw the neighborhood the Gregorys lived in, that I was now officially part of the upper class society. I didn't even think about what that would mean for the school district.

Instead of a rundown, graffitied building like I'm used to, the school consists of a perfectly structured building, surrounded by green grass and sparkling, crack-free windows. Half the cars in the parking lot look brand new, and the clothes everyone wear look fresh off the racks from some absurdly expensive store.

"Are you going to be okay with Lyric showing you around?" Mr. Gregory asks me as he parks the sedan in front of the drop-off section. "Because I can walk you in if you need me to."

"No way," Lyric interrupts as she shoves the door open. "As cool as you are, Uncle Ethan, the last thing he needs is you being all awkward, like you usually are around people."

He shakes his head, but he's not irritated, more like mildly entertained. "All right, I'll pick you three up after school, then."

She nods then jumps out at the same time Kale hops

out his side. They both slam their doors as I reach for my door handle, but then pause, feeling terrified. I usually like to blend in and typically do. But with my gauges, faded black clothes, and worn boots, I'm going to stick out like a sore thumb.

I open my mouth to ask Mr. Gregory if he can take me home, but my door swings open and Lyric snaps her fingers and points for me to get out.

"You'll be just fine," she assures me as if she's read my mind. She slips her bag on then grabs my hand, giving my arm a tug. "I got your back, dude."

I flinch at her touch and almost jerk back. I hate being touched almost as much as I loathe nighttime. But as I catch sight of the abundance of so-called classy people roaming around, I end up clinging on to her as I climb out of the car, oddly grateful that Lyric doesn't let my hand go as we walk up the wide pathway toward the glass entrance centered below a brick archway.

People are staring at us. At me. At me holding Lyric's hand. At my outfit. My piercings. It brings me back to the day we were pulled out of that house while the entire neighborhood watched the three malnourished orphans as if they were part of a freak show they couldn't tear their eyes from.

"God, it's like no one's ever informed them that staring is rude," Lyric mutters as she slams her palm against the glass door and shoves it open.

Pretty much all eyes land on us as we step inside the narrow hallway lined with lockers. Some people look interested. Others repulsed. Some utterly baffled.

Lyric waves to a lot of people and stops to chat with a couple of girls, never releasing my hand. She introduces me to a girl named Maggie, who looks at me like I'm the rebel she wants to walk on the bad side with. The look is nothing new; a lot of girls do it, except Lyric. She just looked at me like she to be my friend.

"Hey, Ayden." Maggie offers me her hand, fluttering her eyelashes. "So, where are you from?"

"Nowhere important." I don't take her offered hand. Don't want to encourage the fluttering of her eyelashes. Don't want to be looked at like that. Don't want to be looked at at all.

When Maggie's eyebrows bow up, Lyric glances at me with her brow cocked. "You'll have to excuse Ayden," she says to Maggie. "He's a man of few words."

"Oh, the sexy silent type," she says, chomping loudly on a piece of gum. "Nice."

"No, just the silent, doesn't like to chat type," I say, switching my weight uncomfortably, wishing Lyric would end the conversation and just take me to the office so I can check in and get the fuck out of this overcrowded, stuffy hall.

"I don't get it." Maggie blinks at Lyric for help.

"It doesn't matter." Lyric waves good-bye before tugging me down the hallway.

"We so need to work on your people skills," she tells me as she steers me through the mob.

"My people skills are fine."

She snorts a laugh. "Okay."

I sigh, giving up on the argument, and instead focus on what's going on around me. Most of the kids look on the preppy side, except for a group lingering around the benches in the quad. I make eye contact with them, figuring they'll be the best start toward finding my place here. But the tallest guy in the group gives me a hard stare in return, and a curvy girl with purple hair flips me the bird.

The day only gets shittier from there. Everyone at this damn school seems to hate me, and the other half seems overly interested. I don't want that. Don't want their stares. I just want to be left alone, since I'll be out of here when the week passes.

I do my best to keep my distance from most people, and spend lunchtime in the bathroom. When fifth period rolls around, though, things really go to shit. It's PE, which is bad enough, but I also have it with Lyric.

"You have been avoiding me," she says as she waltzes up to the bottom bleacher I'm sitting on, waiting for class to start. She has on a red T-shirt and short, black gym shorts that show off her extremely long legs. "What's up with that?"

"When was I avoiding you?" I ask, fiddling with the drawstring on my own shorts.

"At lunch." She sits down beside me and crosses her legs. "I looked everywhere for you. Where the hell were you?"

I pick at a hole in the bottom of my shorts. "I ate in the bathroom."

Her nose crinkles. "Ew, Ayden. No, no, no. Just no."

I shrug. "It was better than being stared at."

"Who's staring at you?"

I give her a '*really*' look.

She sighs. "All right, I'll give you the staring thing." She rests her elbows on the bench behind us and reclines back, staring at the gym floor. "My school has apparently never seen someone so gothically adorable."

"What does that even mean?"

She smirks at me. "You know, dark, mysterious, sullen, yet cute."

I gape at her. "Do you even have a filter?"

She swiftly shakes her head. "No way. Where's the fun in that?"

I continue to stare at her, impressed and kind of afraid of her. She's so open. So honest. So unlike me, the guy who barely speaks and who carries pills with him, contemplating suicide. Lyric is my polar opposite.

"Hey, Lyric." A guy wearing baggie gym shorts and a school T-shirt comes strolling up to us with a smile on his face. "How's it going?"

"Hey, Lanson." Lyric smiles up at him then leans forward to tie her shoe. "Have you met Ayden?"

Lanson's eyes land on me and the friendliness he conveyed when he was staring at Lyric disappears. "Yeah, new guy, right? I think we have English together."

"Yeah, I think so." Heaviness develops in my chest as more attention is focused on me. *God, I wish this day would just get over with.*

"You two should hang out," Lyric suggests with her head still tipped down as she loops her shoelace.

Lanson sneers. "Oh yeah, I'm sure we can be best friends." When Lyric looks up again, his haughtiness turns into a friendly smile. "In fact, I'm having a party this weekend. You two should come."

Lyric glances over her shoulder at me. "What do you think? Are you up for a party?"

Lanson glares at me. I can't tell if he wants me to agree to go or to say no, but one thing's for sure: my existence is clearly irritating him.

I force a tight smile. "Sure, a party sounds fun."

The death glare vanishes from Lanson's face when Lyric looks back at him. "Oh, time for class." Lyric springs up and grabs my hand, hauling me to my feet.

That move earns me the darkest scowl from Lanson. I have a feeling things are going to get a hell of a lot worse.

I wish I could follow Lyric, but the teacher splits up the class—boys on one side, girls on the other. Then we're divided into teams of three and handed a basketball. Athletics was never my thing, but I try my best, even when I start to get criticized by Lanson, who of course has to be on the team I'm playing against.

He smirks at me as he throws the ball over my head to another member of the team then "accidentally" elbows me in the gut.

"Where are you from?" he asks as we both jog down the court toward the ball.

"Nowhere important." I dodge to the right when the ball is thrown again and surprisingly catch it.

My shoe squeaks against the floor as he knocks the ball out of my hand before I can even start dribbling. "One thing's for sure; you sure as hell aren't from here." He stares me up and down as if I'm trash. "I heard you were adopted or some shit. Not sure why the hell anyone would want you." He jabs me in the side with his elbow.

It takes all my strength not to clock him in the face.

"And why the hell is Lyric Scott hanging out with you?" Another elbow rammed to the rib cage, this time with so much force it nearly knocks the wind out of me.

For a brief moment, I tumble into a memory from two years ago. The exact same thing occurred then, only it was an adult who took the air from me. As fast as I fall into the memory, it fizzles out like a flame.

"I mean, I get that she thinks she needs to be friends with everyone," Lanson continues, "but seriously, she's sinking to the bottom of the barrel with you."

When he stomps on my foot, I can't take it anymore. I was taught not to fight back when I was younger, but once I entered the system, all bets were off, and I did pretty much whatever the hell I wanted. I was going to try to be better, though, because the Gregorys seemed genuinely nice, but fuck it.

I push him. "Dude, shut the fuck up."

A shit-eating smirk spreads across his face at my reaction. "Or what?" He inches toward me and gives me a shove back. "What are you going to do about it? Because in case you haven't heard, I'm the shit around here."

"Wow, there's an accomplishment," I retort, regaining my balance. "The shit of Glensview High School. I'm sure that's going to get you far in life."

"Way farther than you," he bites back as he glances at my piercings, black nail polish, and gauges. "Seriously, I bet if they searched your room, they'd find dead animals everywhere."

I inhale and exhale, trying to stay calm. "And if they searched yours, I'm sure they'd find steroids."

His smirk shifts to a scowl. Then he's spinning around to catch the ball, but mid-turn, he brings his elbow up and slams it hard into my face. Blood gushes from my nostrils and pain radiates all the way up to my head as I hunch over, groaning.

Fuck that hurt.

Goddamnit, I hate life.

Life always hurts.

I should have just taken the bottle of pills this morning. Spared myself another day's worth of pain.

I'm about to stand upright and go after him—who gives a shit about the consequences—but then I hear a burst of commotion and someone shouting.

When I glance up, Lanson is on his knees, cupping his own nose, and Lyric's standing in front of him with her hands on her hips.

"Next time, it's going to be my fist, asshole," she says to him then reels around to me. "Are you okay?" She lowers my hands from my nose, wincing at the sight. "We need to get you to the nurse."

"What did you do to him?" My voice sounds all nasal-ly.

"I threw the basketball at his face." She winks at me. "I told you I got your back, dude."

I'm not sure how to respond. No one has ever had my back. Not even my brother and sister, but that wasn't their fault. None of us could take care of ourselves at the time, let alone each other. It feels nice. More than nice. Nice is something new to me. Different. For a moment, I feel different.

And for a fleeting, life-changing moment, I'm kind of glad I didn't take those pills this morning.

Chapter 3

Lyric

"So what happened?" is the first thing Ayden says when I approach his locker after school.

"Not much. I got detention for a few days, but the principal loves me and always goes easy on me." I slide my backpack on. "What about you?"

He shrugs as he retrieves his bag out of his locker and unzips it. "Nothing, really. I went to the nurse. She put some ice on my nose then sent me on my way."

I squint at his nose. "It looks really gnarly."

He touches the brim of it and winces. "It feels really gnarly." He removes a few textbooks out of his locker, stuffing them in his bag. "How much trouble do you think we're going to be in when we get home?"

"You know, I've been putting a lot of thought into that," I say as he slams his locker. "And I've come up with a plan."

"A plan?" he questions as he secures his backpack onto his back. "What kind of plan?"

"Well, the best bet is to play Uncle Ethan right from the start, because he gets really uncomfortable over almost everything." I link arms with him as we start down the busy hall. I've been touching him a lot today, and while I can tell it bothers him, I'm not going to stop until he asks me to. I like touching him. It feels like he's mine, which makes me feel special. "If we can have him convinced that it was an accident right from the start, then we should be good to go when we get home."

"It kind of was an accident," he points out as we exit the doors and enter the deliciously warm sunlight.

"Yeah, but I kind of have a habit of doing stuff like this," I explain as we cross the freshly mowed grass toward the loading area in front of the school. "You'll get off the hook easily, but I might have to do some time."

His arm flexes beneath my touch. "I'm not going to let you get into trouble over this—over me. I'll make sure of that."

"Aw, so you're the hero type." I playfully bump my shoulder into his. "Never would have guessed that about you."

He comes so close to smiling. Just a little more joking,

and I know I can make it happen.

I open my mouth to crack another joke, but snap my jaw shut when I spot the Gregory's gigantic sedan parked amongst the line of cars. "Crap."

"What?" Ayden tracks my gaze to the driver's seat where Aunt Lila is sitting. And in the passenger seat is my mother. "Okay, so now what do we do?"

I overdramatically bobble my head back. "Now, we go face the music."

Aunt Lila is so grateful for my stepping in for Ayden that she actually starts to tear up. She seems heartbroken that someone would want to hurt him. She keeps saying to him, "You've already been through so much. This isn't fair." I can tell Ayden gets really uncomfortable with the waterworks. Thankfully, my mom intervenes and calms Lila down. Then, she turns around in her seat and lays my punishment on me.

The punishment is the stupidest thing ever, though. One week of cleaning my room and one week of hanging out with Ayden after school. Plus, I have to help out at the shelter on Thanksgiving. Like that's a punishment. I have to clean my room anyway and the shelter thing is a tradition.

After we get home, I end up in Ayden's room, sprawled on the bed with the door agape. Lila keeps coming in to check on us, as if she half expects to catch us naked and fondling each other. Fat chance that'll happen. Even though Ayden is ridiculously adorable in a self-tortured artist, gothic, I'm-internally-tortured sort of way, I'm saving myself for someone who will capture my wild soul and tame it. I know I sound like a sap, but I blame it on my parents' undying love story. Even after twenty years of marriage, they're still ridiculously in love, so the bar for my own love story is set pretty high.

"Are you sure you two don't want a snack?" Lila sticks her head into the room for the umpteenth time.

Ayden nods as he situates against the headboard, working on his English assignment. "I'm sure."

She looks at me and I shrug. "I ate a buttload of cookies before I came up here."

"Okay," she says disappointedly then leaves us to get back to our homework.

The soft tune of "Cardiac Arrest" by Bad Suns flows from the stereo as Ayden continues to jot answers down, but. I'm more fixated on him than my assignment.

"So, did the gauges hurt when you got them?" I ask as I doodle thorny vines all over my math paper.

When he glances up from his paper, strands of his black hair hang in his grey eyes. "I don't know. Probably about as bad as your ear piercings."

I touch the rose earrings in my ears then kneel up on the mattress. "What about tattoos?"

"What about them?"

"Do you have any?"

"I'm only sixteen."

"Yeah, so." I arch my back as I stretch. "I bet you do, don't you?" When he wavers, I immediately perk up. "Where are they?"

"There's no they." He sets down the pencil in the spine of the book and flexes his fingers like he has a cramp. "Just one."

"Can I see it?" I eagerly move over to sit down beside him.

His expression plummets. "I don't think ..." He trails off when my mouth sinks. "Fine, I'll show you, but only if you promise not to ask questions."

I draw an X over my chest with my finger. "I promise."

Unraveling You

A nervous exhale escapes his lips as he reaches for the hem of his black T-shirt. Excitement bubbles inside me as he lifts it up and shows me his stomach then his side. Black ink stains his flesh in swirls and patterns that form a jagged circle. The tattoo doesn't look professional by any means. In fact, it looks as though someone branded him with an iron rod then dumped ink into the wound.

"Whoa. Does it mean anything?" I extend my hand forward to touch the tattoo, but he quickly jerks his shirt down.

"I don't know if it does or not, since I can't really remember how it got there," he says coldly. He collects his pencil and returns his book to his lap. "And you promised me you wouldn't ask questions."

He begins working on the assignment again, leaving me with so many questions I feel like I'm going to combust. There's so much I don't know about him, and so much I want to know.

"Can I just learn one tiny thing about you?" I clasp my hands in front of me. "Pretty please. It doesn't have to be about the tattoo." When he sighs, I add, "Okay, I'll tell you something that no one else knows about me first." I deliberate what to divulge. I'm not much of a secret keeper, but there is one thing I never tell anyone. "Okay, so no one knows this, but I totally suffer from stage fright, which is a big, huge problem since I want to be the lead singer in a fucking awesome rock band one day." I pat him on the arm. "See, not so bad. Now it's your turn."

He stares at me with uncertainty.

"Just one thing." I hold a finger up. "That's not so bad, right?"

He considers my proposal, and then in the softest voice admits, "I'm terrified of the dark." His gaze drops to the scars on his hand.

"See, that wasn't so bad." I try to remain cheery even though he looks absolutely horrified that he just admitted that secret to me. "And now I know what to get you for your birthday."

"And what's that?" A frown etches into his face.

I wink at him, hoping to cheer him up. "A nightlight." I settle down in the bed beside him. "Don't worry, I won't tell anyone."

"I wasn't worried about that."

"Then why do you look so upset?"

He shrugs, staring at the foot of the bed. "It's nothing."

His gaze collides with mine, and he gapes at me in bafflement. "It's just ... how can you be so happy all the time?"

His question makes me pause and really think about who I am.

"I'm not that happy, am I?" *Am I?*

"Kind of. I mean, I barely know you, but ... you just smile a lot." I self-consciously bring my fingers to my lips, but he swiftly catches my hand, stopping me. The contact sends fireworks blazing across my skin and makes me want to smile even more. "I don't mean it as a bad thing. I just wish I could ... understand it." His shoulders sag as he removes his hand.

Such a sad boy.

With sad eyes.

And a sad heart.

Sad everything.

Too sad.

I need to make him happy.

Somehow.

"I'll make you smile a lot in the future," I promise him after the silence finally gets to me. "You just wait and see. I will drive you so damn crazy, to the brink of insanity, where all you can do is smile. My form of torture will be lots and lots of jokes that will be so hilarious they'll make you pee your pants."

He snorts a laugh but then his eyes widen.

I thought I was being funny, but maybe I scared him. Some people say I come on too strong.

"I was just kidding," I say. "Sort of."

He searches my eyes, his forehead creasing. "I'll be right back," he mumbles as he scrambles to his feet. He bends over to unzip his bag then digs an orange bottle out before running out of the room.

Okay, maybe I need to tone it down a bit. Perhaps he's not quite ready for my sparkling personality and odd sense of humor.

Tone it down, Lyric.

It's not so complicated.

When he reappears in the doorway, his hands are empty and he seems a bit more relaxed.

"Everything okay?" I cautiously ask as he climbs back onto his bed and opens up his Life Sciences book.

He nods, propping the book on his lap. "Yeah, but could you help me with this assignment?" He avoids eye contact with me, and his fingers tremble as he picks up the pencil. "Science really isn't my thing."

I want to ask him about the bottle. About the fear in his eyes. Crack his head open and see what's inside. Write songs about his inner workings. But I also promised I'd make him smile from now on, and my questions seem to have the opposite effect on him.

So I do what he asks and help him, silently telling myself that one day he'll trust me enough that I'll be able to learn what makes him tick. Then I will write the longest, most meaningful song about everything I've discovered.

Everything about him.

Even his secrets.

Chapter 4

Ayden

I've had the same dream for over two years now. Claws. Bleeding flesh. Scars. Scars. Scars. Pain. Metal. Biting. My Flesh. Over and over again. The images are so vague, yet bright as my mind battles not to fully see what happened to me during that week a couple of years ago.

God, I hate this.

The chains were always the worst. They're what I remember the most. Other details are hazy, though, like the people I met while I was trapped. The people who stole everything from me and my brother and sister.

I thought the dreams would go away once I was adopted, or at least hoped they would. But the memories still haunt me most nights, and sometimes during the day when I'm awake. They're extra worse tonight, probably because tomorrow marks a month since I left the shithole of a home I was in before I ended up at the Gregory's. One month since I started my new life. Yet, even a month later, I worry that when I wake up, my nightmares are reality—that this isn't really my life.

Music is the only thing that can calm me down. Well, that and the crazy black light nightlight Lyric bought me for my birthday a couple of weeks ago. She thought she was being funny when she gave it to me, but I was oddly touched that she remembered my stupid confession about being afraid of the dark.

Fortunately, I never told her why I was afraid. Then again, I don't even know the whole reason since I blocked out most of the darker stuff that happened to me. No matter how hard my therapist tries to unravel my mind, they still refuse to surface.

After turning on the black light, everything white in my room glowing neon, I put in my earbuds then toss and turn for half the night until I fall asleep around two in the morning.

Hours later, I'm woken up out of a nightmare by the soft sound of breathing. And not mine. Someone is lying next to me in bed, and for a moment, I have a panic attack, thinking that somehow I've traveled back in time when I was never alone. Then I catch the faintest scent of strawberries and relax. The person lying next to me is the same person who's been climbing into my bed almost every morning since I moved here.

"Are you awake yet?" Lyric asks, ruffling my hair with her fingers. "I'm getting bored watching you sleep."

"Then stop watching me," I murmur with my eyes shut. "It's creepy."

"Hate to burst your bubble, but you're equally as creepy as I am."

"Guess we're perfect for each other, then."

"Of course we are." She flicks me in the forehead, startling me. My eyelids lift open, my gaze meeting her bright green eyes. They're intense to look at, even now after I've known her for a while. I can never seem to stop staring at them. They're beautiful. And it's heartbreaking to feel what my staring at them means. That I like her. A lot. More than I've liked anyone in a long, long time.

"You're doing that creepy staring thing again," she informs me as she sits up in my bed and starts raveling a strand of her hair around her finger. She's dressed in maroon shorts and a dark grey shirt, clearly ready to go somewhere, and knowing our routine, I'm going with her. "You know, it's cool with me. I get it. I'm too dazzling not to stare at." She smiles and my heart misses a beat. Her smile is so perfect and easy. Most days, I envy it. "But you might want to lay off on the staring a little bit in school, at least around Tina Marlelytone."

"I've never stared at Tina Marlelytone." I sit up in bed and stretch my arms over my head.

"I figured, but she thinks you do. So, you might want to"—she points at my eyes—"keep those sad little puppy dog eyes off her."

My hands drop to my lap as I stare blankly at her. "I wish you'd stop saying that about my eyes."

"I'll stop saying that when it stops being the truth." She jumps off the bed and jerks the blanket off me. "Now get up and get dressed. I have big plans for you today."

"You might want to think before you jerk off the blankets like that," I say to her as I drag my butt out of bed. "One day, I might start sleeping naked."

"I think that'd be more embarrassing for you than it would for me," she retorts, backing toward the door. "You blush when someone sees you with your shirt off."

"That happened one time," I call out, but she ignores me, flashing me a sly grin before closing the door.

Shaking my head, I trudge for the dresser to get some

clothes. Nothing fazes that girl. It's the most terrifying and fascinating thing to observe. And I've observed her, a lot. Everywhere she goes, she finds a crowd and blends in with them, like a freaking chameleon. Me, I'm like a skittish rodent who never feels at ease, always silent and uncomfortable, making everyone around me silent and uncomfortable. Except, of course, Lyric.

I'm extremely lucky to have met her my first day with the Gregorys. I'm not sure I would have survived without her. No one knows how hard that first day with the Gregorys was, and all the ones before that. I pondered suicide, touched many blades to my wrists, tasted the staleness of pills. Then Lyric sprung into my life with her sunshine attitude and smile, and suddenly my days don't seem so dark. I decided the day she beat the crap out of the guy to defend me that I was going to dump the pills and try to give a go at life, the best that I could.

And I've been working on it ever since.

As I'm searching for a shirt, my fingers skate across one of the three objects hidden in the back of the drawer. The stuff I brought here with me. I still haven't been able to get rid of them. I still think about my brother and sister every day, and wonder where they are.

"Are you still naked!" Lyric laughs as she bangs on the door, interrupting my thoughts.

"Just a second." I slam the drawer shut then tug on a grey T-shirt and a pair of holey black jeans. Then I grab my boots from the closet and throw open the door. "You are the most impatient person ever."

She rolls her eyes at me. "Whatever, shy boy. I'm super patient." She seizes my hand and leads me down the hall toward the stairway. "So, it's going to be a little bit tricky to get out of the house, since the usual tradition for the month marker is to spend the day talking and eating cake and ice cream, but I have an idea to get around it."

Sunlight is flowing in through the massive windows of the kitchen, and I detect the scent of freshly baked cake in the air. The smell is starting to become more and more familiar with each day I spend here, just like everything else. While I embrace it, I also fear that it will all be taken away from me.

"Maybe we should just stay here, especially if Mrs. Gregory has baked." It's not just that though. I always feel guilty whenever I'm about to do something even remotely wrong. The Gregorys were kind enough to put a roof over my head, and I constantly feel in debt to them.

Lyric shoots me an inquiring look over her shoulder. "Why do you keep insisting on calling them Mr. and Mrs. Gregory? It's weird."

"I have my reasons," I mutter as I sit down on a stool to put on my boots.

Lyric watches me lace my boots. I know she wants to ask what my reasons are, but she doesn't. That's the thing with Lyric. As crazy and blunt as she is, she'll never press me too hard for information. I'm grateful that she doesn't, because if she did discover certain details about me, she probably wouldn't want to be my friend anymore. And I need her as a friend, more than anything.

She places her hands on her hips. "So, what you're saying is you'd rather stay here and eat cake and listen to old timers tell mildly embarrassing stories, instead of going on an adventure with me?"

"No, that's not what I'm saying at all. I just … feel like it's rude to take off."

"It's not rude. Lila wants you to have fun. I know, because she checks with me all the damn time, always worried about your happiness and wellbeing."

"Well, she *should* worry when I'm around you. Some

of the crazy stuff we do … I'm surprised we haven't gotten into trouble yet."

"Give us time." She nudges my foot with hers when I frown at her. "I'm kidding. Everything we do is safe."

Safe?

The word still feels so foreign to me.

Nothing like the word *fear*.

Fear is like air.

Breathable.

Because I know it.

I fear the things I don't know.

Like friendship.

And losing it.

Loss.

Like the loss of my memory.

My childhood.

I lace my boot up then stand up, and she has to angle her chin to look up at me.

"Fine, I'll go with you, as long as you promise that I'll come back in one piece for Mrs. Gregory's sake." I don't know why, but the woman seems to like me. Everyone in the house does, even though I rarely talk.

"All right, getting you back in one piece is doable," Lyric muses then spins around and runs through the kitchen, swiping up a dab of frosting from the cake on her way around the island.

We find Mrs. Gregory in the living room, and after a little bit of persuasion—mostly from Lyric—she lets us go.

"Just be careful," Mrs. Gregory says, moving in toward me with her arms out, as if she's going to hug me. Like always, I tense and she promptly backs away. "And be safe, please." She smiles, but it's laced with concern.

I'm still getting used to the whole caring-about-my-wellbeing thing, so I hesitate as my mind catches up with the scene and the emotions connected to it.

I nod then clear my throat and lower my voice so Lyric won't hear me. "Um, I've been meaning to ask you if you found out how my brother and sister are doing."

Sympathy masks her expression. "I'm sorry, sweetie, but I couldn't find anything out. They said the files were confidential." She comfortingly places a hand on my shoulder. "Maybe when they're eighteen we can start looking again. It'll be more possible to find them then."

Smashing my lips together, I nod then rush after Lyric and out the front door before Mrs. Gregory says anything further.

My chest is still pressurized from last night's dream, and now the whole thing with my brother and sister bears down on me. But after we've been in the fresh air for a few minutes, the pressure starts to alleviate. Always does. Houses do that to me. Rooms. Walls. Confinement.

"All right, here's what I'm thinking," Lyric announces as we hike up the driveway toward the open garage of her house. "Today, we are going to fly."

I gape at her. "In case you haven't noticed, people can't fly."

She grins back at me. "Oh, ye of little faith." She squeezes into the garage between the two ridiculously awesome cars that belong to her parents, ones I long to touch, but have never worked up the courage to.

I notice she has an iPod tucked in her back pocket that I'm sure will serve some sort of purpose later on. When she emerges again, she has her bike.

"We're going to take this bad boy down to Cherry Hill."

"No way. That hill is freaking steep. Plus, aren't we a little too old for bikes?"

"We are never too old for bikes." She juts out her lip. "Pretty please. With a cherry on top."

It's really hard not to say yes to her when she looks like that. Still, I'm torn between coming back to Mrs. Gregory in one piece and making Lyric happy.

"All right, I'll do it, as long as we wear helmets. And take my bike."

"I'll agree to the helmets, but we have to take my bike. Yours doesn't have pegs."

"Why do we need pegs?"

A mischievous grin lights up her face, and I know I'm in for something really iffy when we reach that hill. "You'll see."

Ten minutes later, I'm riding a purple bike, wearing a helmet, and Lyric is standing on the back pegs. She has her hands placed on my shoulders, and I'm both content and uneasy about the touch—always am.

"Okay, stop the bike right here," she says, pointing over my shoulder at the center of the street on top of Cherry Hill.

I aim the bike in the direction and plant my feet onto the asphalt when we arrive at the spot. The inclined road, bordered with lofty, narrow homes, makes me dizzy.

"Are you sure about this?" I warily eye the bottom of the hill, which is an intersection.

Nodding, she pops an earbud into my ear while placing one in her own. "I have to do this, Ayden. It's important to my musical inspiration."

As the lyrics of "Fire Fire" by Flyleaf fill my head, I summon a deep breath, pick up my feet, and position them on the pedals. I don't even have to put pressure on them. The bike takes off on its own and descends quickly down the hill, gaining momentum the further down we go. I start to grow nervous, and my nerves only escalate when Lyric's hands leave my shoulders.

"What the heck are you doing?" I peek back at her while grasping onto the handlebars.

"Flying." She has her arms spanned out to the side, her head angled toward the sky. Her long blonde hair blows out behind her as the wind dances through it. Moments later, she shuts her eyes.

Everything pauses. The freedom she carries is a beautiful, enthralling sight. So enthralling that it feels like I'm falling …

"Ayden, look out!" Lyric shouts, her eyes wide open as

her hands clamp down on my shoulders.

I look at the road just in time to see a car heading at us. I swerve to the left, but it doesn't help as we barrel toward a thick tree. The front wheel of the bike slams into the truck and I go soaring over the handlebars. Thankfully, I manage to keep my head from hitting the concrete, because even with the helmet on, it would have hurt like a motherfucker. The wind gets knocked out of me, though, and I struggle for oxygen as I lie on my back, staring up at the sky, feeling strangely free at the moment, even with the pain.

"Oh my God. Oh my God. Oh my God." Lyric appears above me, worry written all over her face as she throws her helmet off. "Be okay. Be okay. Be okay." She frantically scans my face and then my body, checking for wounds.

Honestly, I feel fine. My knee and elbow ache a bit, but that's it. I've experienced way more pain than this. I remain still, though, fascinated with how fussy she's being. Normally she's so carefree, but right now she's wound up and panicking. Over me.

I've lived with over six families, and no one has ever cared about me as much as Lyric appears to right now.

Soft lyrics flow through my head.

Let me sing you to sleep.

76

Kiss your pain away.

Take your next breath for you.

And keep it as my own forever.

Maybe I'm an asshole for doing it, but I pretend to be hurt, lying still for longer than I should, seeking the fussing just a bit longer. When her eyes meet mine again, I start to feel bad for causing her so much worry. I open my mouth to tell her I'm okay, but the intense look on her face causes me to burst out laughing.

When her eyes narrow, I raise my hands, surrendering. "I'm sorry. I swear. I was just messing around. I'm fine. I promise."

She pinches my arm and I wince, yet continue laughing.

"Seriously, Ayden. That's not funny."

"Oh, come on." I prop up onto my elbows. "Don't pretend like you wouldn't have done the exact same thing."

She crosses her arms, trying to remain pissed, but Lyric never stays upset for more than five seconds, and right on time, she relaxes. "Okay, I'll let you off the hook, but only because I got you to smile." She smiles herself as I reach up and touch my upturned lips.

She's right. I am smiling. And laughing. It's been such a long time that I hadn't even noticed.

"Come on." She stands up, brushes some of the grass off her legs, then offers me her hand. "Let's move on to phase two."

"Phase two?" I question with doubt.

"What, you don't trust me?"

The mangled bike ten feet away should answer that question for me. Regardless of the bent metal and dents in the frame, I still wholly trust her. More than I've trusted anyone.

I nod, lace my fingers through hers, and get to my feet. "But no more hills."

"Deal." She grins.

The day feels so perfect. So real. I just wish I knew if my brother and sister have the same thing.

Chapter 5

Ayden

We spend the rest of the day doing things a little less dangerous, rolling the mangled bike along with us. We walk down to the local bridge, go get some ice cream, and hang out at the park for a while. By the time we arrive back home, the sun has lowered and the sky is black.

As we're putting the bike away in the garage, Lyric checks her phone. "Oh, looks like we have the place to ourselves. Everyone went out to the movies."

"What are we going to do? Because I know you're already thinking of something."

"You know me way too well."

As she ponders an idea, I dare to touch the shiny black Chevelle in the garage. I remember how one of my foster fathers had one similar to it, only it needed a lot more work. He was one of the mildly tolerable parental figures. He never did let me touch the car, though.

"You know, I could always ask my mom if you can drive it," she unexpectedly says.

I hastily withdraw my hand from the car, as if I've been caught with my hand in the cookie jar. "No, I'm okay."

"Well, you can drive mine when I get it, then. It's going to be a Dodge Challenger, though. And a fixer upper. At least, that's the plan we've had since I turned fifteen and a half and got my driving permit." When I look at her again, she's got her evil plan face on. "So, do you want to see something really cool?"

"Maybe," I reply cautiously. "It really depends on what it is."

Grinning deviously, she guides me through the house, toward the back section, coming to a halt at a closed door beside the den.

"I've never been in this room before," I remark as her fingers encase the doorknob.

"That's because I'm technically not allowed in here unless my dad's with me."

Before I can protest, she shoves open the door and flips on the light.

All of my objections abruptly dissipate.

"This is your dad's office?" I step over the threshold behind her and glance around the room filled with old guitars, signed albums, drumsticks, photos, and plaques. So much cool stuff my mind goes into overload.

"More like his memorabilia room." She strolls over to a shelf lined with old CDs and starts tracing her fingers along the rows, reading the titles.

I shut the door then stand in the middle of the room, afraid to touch anything. "Maybe we shouldn't be in here."

"We'll be fine as long as we put everything back in its rightful place." She pulls a CD off the shelf, plucks the disc out, then gently places it into a stereo and presses play. Moments later, a grungy song fills the speakers.

"What band is this?" I ask as I roam around the room, examining all the guitars on the walls.

She shrugs as she plops down in the chair behind the desk and collects a guitar propped against the wall. "The front of the CD cover says The Cranberries. I just randomly picked it. Thought a surprise would be fun." She strums a few notes. "I'm wondering if it was one of my mother's CDs, though." Her lips part as if she's going to sing, and her eyes drift shut. But instead of belting out the lyrics, she plays the notes while uttering the words under her breath. When she opens her eyes again, she looks nervous, which is strange. Lyric never, ever looks nervous.

"You okay?"

She nods, setting the guitar aside. "Yeah, just seeing if I could do it around you."

"Do what around me?"

She shrugs as she opens a drawer. "Sing."

I wish I could help her get over her fear, but unlike what she did for me, I can't just buy her a nightlight.

"What were you whispering to Aunt Lila about this morning?" she casually asks as she sifts through a stack of papers on the desk.

"Nothing important." I plop down in a swivel chair in front of the desk and start spinning in circles.

"I heard you say something about your brother and sister." She reads something on one of the papers, but I can tell she's pretending, worried she's crossing a line. "I didn't know you had a brother and sister."

"I did ... before ..." I pick up the pace, whirling the chair around and around until I'm so dizzy I feel like I'm going to hurl. "My brother is a year older than me and my sister is a year younger."

"And you haven't seen them since you had to leave your home?"

"No."

"Does it make you sad, that you all had to leave your home and now you don't get to see them?"

I dig my heels into the floor and stop the chair before I actually do end up vomiting. She's watching me intently, waiting for me to answer, with a drop of apprehension in her eyes.

"I don't miss my old ... home at all," I utter quietly. "It wasn't even a home ... at least, from what I can remember ... but I do miss my brother and sister. That's why I asked Mrs. Gregory if she could find stuff out about them—or at least where they are."

Her head angles to the side and she looks so lost. "You said from what you can remember."

"Huh?" My voice is thick with emotion. Just talking about this is surfacing unwanted memories that are supposed to be forgotten.

"Just barely, you said, 'from what I can remember.'" She shifts in her seat, leaning back. "Can you not remember your old home?"

Seeing no other way out of this than to lie to her—which I won't do—I nod. "Some of my memories are foggy."

"Does Mrs. Gregory know about this?"

"Vaguely. I think social services and the therapist I've been going to told her some details." I clench my fists as my chest starts to constrict.

Links of metal wrapped around my wrist and brain.

Driving me insane.

Begging me to cave.

They whispered they knew the truth.

Marked it forever on my flesh.

Told me to give in.

To surrender.

But I couldn't.

I blink from my thoughts and massage my wrists.

"Maybe I could help you find them," she says, thrumming her fingers on top of the desk.

"Who?"

"Your brother and sister."

"And how would we do that"—my fingers curl around the armrest, desperate to hold onto something, because I feel like I'm about to have a panic attack—"when Mrs. Gregory couldn't even find them?"

She slants forward, crossing her arms on top of the

desk. "There's a little thing called the internet, Ayden. We could do some research on our own."

"You would help me do that?"

"I would help you do anything."

Even though the concept doesn't feel possible, I believe her. "Where would we start?"

Her eyes elevate to the ceiling as she contemplates. "You know their last names, right?"

I nod. "My brother's name is Felix, and my sister's name is Sadie. Our last name used to be Stephorson, but I'm not sure now if theirs still is, since mine's changed."

"Okay, we can start there. And it'd probably help if they had something distinct about them."

My fingers travel to the homemade tattoo on my side, put there without my permission. "They have the same tattoo as me."

Her lips part, but no words come out. I've shocked Lyric beyond words, which doesn't seem natural.

"We didn't choose to get them," I mumble, completely clueless why I'm telling her this. "They were put on us, from what I can remember."

She sucks her bottom lip into her mouth, as if she's

trying to physically restrain herself from asking.

"What happened to you?" she finally asks.

I grind my teeth so forcefully it actually hurts my jaw. "When I was younger, we were taken by these ... people who had these really strange beliefs. They put the tattoos on us." My voice quivers almost as intensely as my heart as I speak of the day my mother betrayed her three children. It's the same day that my memories start to break apart into charred fragments that barely make sense.

Lyric swallows hard. "Ayden ... I ..."

"Can we please talk about something else now?" I plead in desperation, barely able to breathe. "Please. Something happy." I need my happy Lyric back. Need my happiness before I fall back into the darkness that I carried around for two years after that day.

Silence stretches between us before Lyric says, "Did you hear about Maggie?"

I exhale, my muscles loosening. "No, but I'm guessing she's dating someone new now."

She smiles as she rests back in the chair, making the shift of attitude so breezy. "How'd you guess?"

I give a half shrug. "Because she dates someone new every day."

Lyric giggles, but her laughter silences as she opens the desk drawer. She squints at something inside it, and a pucker forms at her brow. "What on earth?" She pulls out a bottle of scotch along with a pack of cigarettes and an ashtray. "Dude, I know my parents drink"—she shows me the pack of cigarettes—"but I never knew they smoked."

"I'm not surprised. I've smelled it on your dad before." I stretch my legs out and slant my head back at the ceiling decorated with hundreds of guitar picks. "It must have been so cool growing up here," I remark as I spin the chair around, imagining what it was like living here. Probably pretty great since she's so damn happy all the time.

"Yeah, I guess it was pretty fucking awesome." Lyric unexpectedly starts hacking.

My gaze darts to her. I have to bite my lip to restrain my laughter. "Did you just take a drink of that?"

She wipes her lips, shuddering as she stares at the bottle of scotch in her hand. "Yeah, so what?"

"Have you ever drank before?"

"No." She twists the cap back on. "Have you?"

I shrug. "A couple of times." That's all I say, not wanting to relive the things I've done, like fighting, drinking,

Jessica Sorensen

and stealing stuff. "You shouldn't start with scotch. That's strong shit right there."

She meticulously eyes me over. "You want a taste?" She extends her arm across the desk, with her fingers enclosed around the bottle.

Even though I probably shouldn't, I snatch the bottle from her and swallow a gulp or two as Lyric watches me with inquisitiveness. When I remove the mouth of the bottle from my lips, she grins.

"You didn't even gag." She grabs a cigarette, along with a lighter that's inserted into the pack.

"I wouldn't do that if I were you. He'll be able to smell it."

"I'm just curious." She reclines back in the chair and pops the end of the cigarette into her mouth.

"Well, you shouldn't be. That stuff is bad for you."

"I'm not curious about smoking," she says, cupping her hand around her face as she flicks the lighter and tries to light the end, "but about you."

"What are you talking about?"

"I can never figure stuff out about you."

"Like what? If I know how to light a lighter?"

She shakes her head, still struggling to light the cigarette. "No. Like what you like to do. If you really are a bad boy at heart. If you've ever smoked before."

I elevate my brows at her. "That's what you want to know about me? Out of all things?" *After the conversation we just had?*

Giving up on the lighter, she rises from the chair and ambles around the desk toward me with the cigarette still resting between her lips. "Well, I have this theory that this good, obedient guy I know isn't the guy who pulled up in that sedan a month ago." She leans over me and taps the hollow of my neck. "I mean, the collar's gone. You took it off at day three, and I could never figure out why—why it was so easy for you to give up your Goth side." She slides her hand to my ear and traces her finger across the lobe, moving her body close enough that I get a straight view down the front of her shirt. I try not to look, but my eyes stray more than a few times, my heart rate quickening. "And the gauges, too. All you have now are these tiny scars." Her hands travel down my arms, causing goose bumps to sprout across my skin as her fingers come to a rest on the tops of my hands. I start to panic, thinking she's going to ask me about the scars there; instead, she grazes the pad of her thumb over my fingernail. "I really do kind of miss the black nail polish."

I shiver from her touch. "I don't." My voice cracks as her fingers graze my knuckles, and I quickly clear my throat.

It's just a simple touch.

A lyrical brush of fingers.

Nothing that can hurt you.

Anymore.

All thoughts vanish, when she straddles my lap. My heart slams forcefully against my chest. I can't figure out what to do with my hands. Definitely not touch her; otherwise, I might lose it. But I look awkward with them out to the side, so I drape them on the armrests and fold my fingers inward.

"How much of that did you drink?" I inspect her face to see if she could possibly be drunk, but I'm feeling a little woozy myself and my vision is a bit hazy.

"A few swallows." She hands me the lighter, places the cigarette in between her lips again, and waits for me to light it for her.

"This is going to teach you a lesson." I drag my thumb across the top of the lighter and bring the flame closer to the cigarette.

"And what lesson is that?" she asks as the fire crinkles the paper. Moments later, she begins hacking again. She hurriedly removes the cigarette from her mouth as clouds of smoke puff from her lips.

"That smoking is bad for you." I pry the cigarette from her fingers and slant over to put it out in the ashtray, fighting back my laughter.

After she finishes coughing up her lungs, she settles into my lap again. "So have you?"

Again, I question how drunk I am when I start to get a little too happy down south about her sitting on my lap. I've never really been turned on before, not in a welcomed way anyway.

"You're not going to let this go, are you?" I ask, getting squirmy.

She shakes her head, positioning a hand on each side of me. "Nope. Not unless you start freaking out."

I mentally chant the lyrics of the first song I can think of.

You make me dizzy. You make me ache.
You make me burn, burn, burn.

Your touch is toxic. Poison.

Yet I'll never learn, learn, learn.

"Fine," I admit. "Yes, I've smoked before, but not since I moved in with the Gregorys. I went through this phase where I did a lot of things, right after I entered the system."

"I knew it." She sloppily plays with my hair, running her fingers through it. "You were a bad, bad boy, Ayden. Maybe that's what I should start calling you. Bad boy instead of shy boy."

"Is that what you're into now? Bad boys?" My voice comes out deeper than I planned.

"Maybe."

"It's a good thing I'm not one anymore, then, huh?"

Her green eyes sparkle as she taps a finger on her bottom lip. "So, you're saying you don't want me to be into you?" I remain silent, feeling as though I might be walking into a trap. Her lips curve upward as she continues, "Because something might suggest otherwise."

A beat of confusion passes until her insinuating gaze drifts downward. Realization clicks.

"Fuck." I hop out from under her so quickly she ends up falling onto the floor. I face the door, cursing under my breath, completely fucking mortified. How the hell did we go from talking about my past to her teasing me about getting a hard-on? I shouldn't be surprised, though. This is Lyric. Make me crazy, ache, trouble breathing, heart-liberating Lyric.

"Don't worry," she says with an off pitch giggle. "It happens to most guys. At least, that's what they taught us in health class."

I shake my head, telling myself to chill the fuck out. *It's not a big deal. It's just Lyric. It doesn't mean anything. Mean* that. "You seriously have no boundaries."

"Yeah, but that's what you love about me."

I can hear her moving up behind me. I have no idea what's about to happen, or what I want to happen. Thankfully, I don't have to think about it too hard, because a door slams from somewhere in the house.

"Oh shit." Lyric flies into panic mode, running over to the desk where the scotch, cigarettes, and ashtray are. She tosses the bottle and cigarettes into the drawer then stares wide-eyed at the ashtray. "What do I do with this?"

Part of me wants to keep my lips zipped to pay her back for teasing me, but I care about her too much to let her get in trouble. So I rush over and grab the ashtray while Lyric turns off the music and stuffs the CD back into place. I carefully open the window and pour the ashes out onto the back lawn. After closing the window, I return the ashtray to the drawer where I find a can of air freshener. I douse the air with it and tell Lyric to flip on the ceiling fan. We finish cleaning up the best we can, and then Lyric seizes my hand and jerks me out the door.

"Just play it cool," she whispers loudly. I can smell the scotch on her breath.

This is a disaster in the making.

"Just let me do the talking," I tell her as we creep up the hall toward the kitchen. "And don't breathe on anyone."

She gives an exaggerated nod. I sigh.

We are so going down.

The situation only worsens when we enter the kitchen. There is cake, ice cream, and plates all over the countertops. Not only are her parents there, but so is every member of the Gregory family, most of them turning to look at us as we enter. I swear to God it's like they know. Mr. Gregory pauses the longest, his head cocking to the side as he searches both our faces.

Fuck, he knows.

I open my mouth to say something, but Lyric beats me to the punch.

"I think I'm going to throw up." Her fingers slip from my hand as she bolts out of the kitchen toward the bathroom.

Mrs. Scott glances at Mr. Scott, and then she runs after Lyric. Mrs. Gregory looks at me, the disappointment in her eyes making me want to sink into the earth and vanish into the dirt. She sighs then whispers something to Mr. Gregory. His eyes widen slightly as she backs away and ushers the kids out of the kitchen with her.

Then it's just Mr. Gregory, Mr. Scott, and I, in an overly large kitchen that somehow feels overcrowded. The situation is alarmingly uncomfortable. Rarely does Mr. Gregory have to be the disciplinarian, but I have a feeling he's about to.

I want to run out the door. Run away. A year ago, I would have, but I don't think I can do it now—go back in the system. No, I'm going to have to grovel, beg them to let me stay here with them.

"I'm sorry, we just …" I trail off, unsure of what to say. The last thing I want to do is get Lyric in trouble, but

I'm worried if I take the fall, I'll be kicked out.

Mr. Scott and Mr. Gregory exchange a look then Mr. Scott scoots out the barstool beside the one he's sitting on and pats the seat while Mr. Gregory leans back against the counter and waits for me sit down.

Blowing out a breath, I plant my ass in the seat.

"What exactly were you and my daughter up to tonight?" Mr. Scott asks, watching me like a hawk.

"Um, we went on a bike ride, sir," I answer, but it sounds more like a question than a response.

"What did you do when you got home, though?" This time it's Mr. Gregory that speaks. "Because if I didn't know any better, I'd guess the two of you have been drinking tonight, which would be really, really bad since we set ground rules of no drinking."

"Um ..." I struggle for a response, glancing back and forth between them.

Rat out Lyric? Get kicked out? What the hell do I do?

I don't want to go back into the system.

Don't want to go back.

Don't want to.

Ever.

Mr. Scott leans over and sniffs the air. "Is that my

scotch I smell on your breath?"

"I'm sorry, sir." My pulse pounds as I rise from the stool with my head tipped down and my shoulders sagging. "I'll go pack my stuff."

"Pack your stuff?" Mr. Gregory mumbles, confused. The two of them trade a look, and then their expressions soften. "Ayden, we're not going to kick you out, if that's what you're getting at."

My gaze skims back and forth between them. "But I broke the rules."

Mr. Gregory says to Mr. Scott, "See, this is what happens when they give us responsibilities. We fuck things up." Shaking his head, he returns his attention to me, standing up straight. "Son, we're not going to kick you out because you broke a rule, but I do need to punish you." He seems puzzled over what to do next, and seeks help from Mr. Scott. "What do I punish him with?"

He shrugs. "I have no fucking idea. Ella usually comes up with the punishments, and this is the first time Lyric's done something like this. Maybe ground him for a week?"

This is the strangest thing I've ever witnessed. In the past homes I lived in, by this point, I'd be getting yelled at.

If I were still at my mother's, fists would have been flying. But that still wouldn't have been the worst part. No, that would come later.

Mr. Gregory considers the idea. "That seems doable." He turns to me. "What do you think?"

I shrug, so damn confused. "Um, it sounds good to me, sir."

He nods, looking relieved as he stands up straight. "All right, you're not allowed to do anything for a week."

I keep my head down as I breathe in relief. "Okay, sir."

"And stop calling me sir," he sternly adds. "That's part of your punishment, too. From now on, you have to call me Ethan."

I'm relieved he didn't ask me to call him dad. That I couldn't handle, since I've never called anyone dad before. Getting kicked out I can't handle either, not anymore. Hell, I can barely handle the fact that they seem to want me around, despite the fact I've messed up.

"Okay." As I'm starting to relax, Mrs. Scott enters the room, dragging Lyric in with her.

"Your daughter would like to tell both of you something," she says, staring at a very pale looking Lyric.

Lyric sighs then looks at her dad. "I'm sorry that I

drank some of your scotch and smoked your secret cigarettes." Her dad's eyes widen, as if he's been busted, while Lyric continues, "And, Mr. Gregory, you should know that it was my idea. I talked Ayden into going into my father's office and into drinking. And he didn't smoke. That was all me." When her gaze flicks over at me, the damn girl smiles and winks.

I got your back, she mouths as she wanders around the counter and takes a seat beside me. She leans in and whispers in my ear, "I'm going to make this up to you by helping you find your brother and sister. I promise."

I want to hug her, but decide it's probably not the best move right now, nor am I sure I can handle a hug. It's a strange feeling, though—wanting to touch someone. It makes me pause. Really think. About who I'm turning into. Could I somehow, after what I've been through, turn out normal? Lose the fear of touching someone? Of the dark? Of the past?

I stay put until eventually everyone gathers back into the kitchen to eat cake and ice cream, and reminisce about my first month as being part of the family. It's a pretty good ending to the day, and part of me thinks the perfection is going to carry throughout the night. That maybe my nightmares will somehow vanish.

But the moment I close my eyes to go to sleep, I fall into darkness and my scars start to bleed again.

Bleed. Bleed. Bleed.

Like wilting rose petals.

Against the darkness.

Dripping against the shadows.

Around me. All around me.

The metal bites my skin.

Killing me slowly. Painfully.

Never letting me breathe again.

Chapter 6
Ayden

Lyric being Lyric, she keeps her promise to me and helps me search for my brother and sister. We spend a lot of time during the summer and well into the beginning of senior year searching. We keep our efforts from the Gregorys and Scotts, though, mainly because it feels like we're doing something wrong.

No article or search gives us any information on their whereabouts, though, even when we try to break into the social service's records—yeah, we're that awesome. Of course, we fail epically with our hacking since neither of us are computer geniuses.

We've been in my room all day. It's late. The stars and moon are shining brightly from outside the window. I'm tired of staring at the computer screen. Lyric looks bored as hell, lying on her stomach on my bed, messing around with her phone.

"I think I need a break," I tell her, swiveling in the chair as I rub my weary eyes.

"Don't get discouraged." Lyric tosses her phone aside and rolls off the bed, tugging the hem of her dress down.

The fabric is black and red with stars on it and it's just the right length that I get an eyeful every time she bends over. I try not to look when she does, but ever since the incident in her father's office a few months ago, I've been struggling with my attraction to her, something I've yet to tell anyone about, even my therapist.

If I were a better guy, I'd tell her to be more careful when she bends over. But I'm not a better guy. I'm a confused guy who got his first welcomed hard-on while she was sitting on his lap. I want her, yet I'm afraid to want her, afraid to feel that way about her, so I try not to look.

"I'm not discouraged." My fingers fall to the keyboard. "I just need a break. I'm bored."

"You're bored. Wow, that's a first." She comes up behind me and places her hands on my shoulders, digging her fingertips into my shirt, massaging my muscles. I tense from her touch, momentarily forgetting how to breathe as her scent immerses me. "You're usually so uptight. You need to relax, dude." She rests her chin on my head as she keeps rubbing, driving my body into a confusion infused frenzy.

"What's up with the constant dude remark?" I ask as I click off the computer screen. "You're always calling me that."

"That's because you're my dude, buddy, bro." She laughs then kisses the top of my head. "Now get up. If you want a break, I'm totally going to give you a break."

"Where are we going to go?" I stand up and stretch my arms above my head, hyper aware that her eyes wander to the bottom of my shirt when it rides up, checking me out.

I feel slightly better about the whole dress thing, but at the same time guilty. And afraid. So fucking afraid all the time, like I have no clue what to do with my emotions for her.

She bites her bottom lip before blinking up at me. "Hmm ... let me think. Somewhere adventurous, of course." She taps her finger to her bottom lip. "How about the Silver Box? I haven't been there in forever, and I heard there was a few cool bands playing tonight."

"But what if it's noisy and crowded?"

"Don't worry. I'll hold your hand." Her bottom lip pops out as she peers up at me through her eyelashes, using the move she recently learned that gets her way. "Pretty please, come with me."

Sighing, I retrieve my hoodie from the back of the computer chair. "Fine, but I need to talk to Lila about my brother first."

She scoops up her leather jacket from the bedpost. "Why? You're not letting her in on our plan, are you?"

I slip my arms through the sleeves then zip up the jacket. "No. But he turns eighteen in a couple of days, and she said it might be easier to find him then."

"I hope so." She slides her jacket on and opens the bedroom door. "Now, let's get this party on the road."

She links arms with me and we head down to the kitchen. When we stroll in, Kale and Everson are sitting at the kitchen table, eating fruit and arguing about sports.

Everson is more reserved, like me, but freaks out over anything that has to do with football, like now as he talks animatedly about some touchdown by the Minnesota Vikings, one of his favorite teams.

Kale seems mildly interested, but still argues with him. He's always kind of marched to the beat of his own drum, wearing a lot of comic book inspired attire, but thankfully, after he turned fifteen a couple of months ago, he stopped with the capes.

"Hey, have you two seen your mom and dad?" Lyric asks, stealing an apple from the fruit basket on the table.

Everson scowls at her. "Jesus, make yourself at home, Lyric. You can't just come eat our food and interrupt our conversation."

Kale, who's usually a talker, freezes mid-bite of his orange slice, and stares at Lyric with his jaw hanging open as she bites into the apple. I have a theory that the poor kid might have a crush on her, since the mouth agape trait is a common thing when Lyric's in his sight.

"Sorry, Everson," Lyric says, stifling a smile as she wipes a trail of juice from her chin.

"We were talking football," Everson tells her, like it explains his rude behavior.

"Okay. Chillax. I just asked a question, which you never did answer." Lyric skims back and forth between the two of them. "Do either of you know where your mom and dad are?"

Annoyed, Everson points over his shoulder toward the living room. "They're in there, whispering secrets about Ayden. They think they're being sneaky about it, but we heard them when we walked by."

I trade a puzzled look with Lyric, and then we simultaneously duck out of the room and make a beeline for the
living room. I'm about to walk right in, but Lyric throws
out her arm and pushes me back behind the wall. Then, she
places her finger to her lips, shushing me as she huddles
against me, leaning to the side to eavesdrop.

I sigh, torn between letting Lyric listen, and not feeling
guilty about doing so myself.

"I'm worried the therapy isn't helping," Lila says con-
cernedly. "He's still saying he can't remember anything.
And he's been pretty adamant about searching for his
brother and sister."

"Baby, I know you want to fix everything, including
the world," Ethan tells her, "but you might just have to ac-
cept that he may not ever remember. Maybe it's good for
him, too. Maybe whatever happened to him is best left in
the dark."

"Yeah, but what about finding his brother and sister?
What am I supposed to do about that?"

"You try to find them," Ethan replies simply. "If he
wants to find them, then he'll find them whether you help
him out or not."

"Yeah, you're probably right." She pauses. "I worry

about him, though. There's still so much he doesn't know—that no one knows."

A stretch of silence goes by, and then they start chatting about Kale and his problems at school. I don't even realize I've gripped onto Lyric's hand until her thumb grazes the inside of my wrist.

What Lila and Ethan were talking about is nothing I don't already know, but hearing the worry in their voices makes me concerned that I might be more messed up than I thought.

"Hey, are you okay?" Lyric asks, searching my eyes with apprehension.

I nod, forcing down the lump in my throat. "Yeah, I'm fine." I free her hand from my death grip and walk into the living room, cleaning off my damp palms on the front of my jeans.

They're both sitting on the sectional, the television is on, but the volume is down, and a lamp is on. There are stacks of papers and receipts piled on the table, armrests, floor, everywhere really, probably for Ethan's outdoor touring business, or Lila's part-time catering business she runs on the weekends.

"Oh, hey, sweetie." Lila and Ethan appear uneasy at my appearance. She has a bright pink mug in her hand that matches her shirt. When she notes Lyric and I are wearing our jackets, she sets the mug down on the coffee table. "I thought you two were hanging out in your room tonight?"

"We were." I exchange a glance with Lyric. "But we got bored and were wondering if we could go to the Silver Box for a while."

Lila looks at Ethan for his input, but he just shrugs. Her gaze glides to the window across the room. "It's pretty late for a school night."

"We won't stay out for too long," Lyric steps in. "There's supposed to be some really cool bands playing tonight."

Ethan straightens up at this. "Yeah, I actually heard that, too."

Lyric's green eyes start to sparkle, and I know she's already conjuring up a plan. "Hey, here's an idea. How about you and my dad go with us? That could be fun."

Ethan rubs his jawline, musing over the idea. "That actually could be fun." He drops the papers he was holding down onto the couch cushion and turns to Lila. "What do you think?"

Lila sighs as she collects her mug, reclines back in the sofa, and crosses her legs. "Go have fun. Just don't keep them out too late."

When Ethan hurries upstairs to get ready, Lyric faces me. "I probably should go make sure my dad is down. Meet you at my garage in like ten?"

I nod.

She gives me a pressing look before walking out of the room. I know her well enough by now to understand that the only reason she left was to give me an opportunity to speak with Lila. I'm just not sure what I want to say anymore, so I end up sticking to my original plan.

"Um, I kind of wanted to ask you something else." I lower myself onto the edge of the coffee table and pick at a hole in my jeans. "I was wondering if we could start looking for my brother again, since his eighteenth birthday is in a few days."

"I was actually expecting you to ask that sooner, and was planning on visiting social services next week." She smiles as she raises the brim of the mug to her lips, but beneath the mask of happiness is uneasiness.

I'm just not sure what the uneasiness is over. Finding

my brother? Or me?

***

I didn't understand why Lyric was so easygoing about bringing her father and Ethan with us to a club, but I quickly find out once I arrive at her house. After some persuading, she convinces Mr. Scott to drive his Chevelle and to let us drive her mother's GTO so we can race to the club. It's a fairly easy win, though, since Mr. Scott seems to go easy on her.

When we arrive at the building secured in the heart of the town, I learn another reason why Lyric was so enthusiastic over taking the parentals. Mr. Scott is a well enough known musician that he gets easy access through the entrance. We stroll right up to the rope where the bouncer waves us in.

A crowd is already forming around the stage, even though we're here early. The air is hot, suffocating, along with the bodies pressed up against me. The mob is thickening at such a rapid rate that we end up losing track of Mr. Scott and Ethan. I just about get split apart from Lyric, too, but fortunately she presses her back against my chest, grabs hold of my hands, and then wraps them around her waist.

I momentarily seize up by her nearness, but then I realize the alternative—let her go and get eaten up by the throng. I grip onto her and hold on for dear life.

Her hair smells amazing, like strawberries with a hint of perfume. The strands tickle my cheeks, causing my eyelashes to lower.

"Are you okay?" she asks over her shoulder as she stares at the stage where the band members have started to set up.

I force my eyelids open. "Yeah, I'm fine. Why?"

Her shoulders lift as she shrugs. "I just wanted to make sure you were okay after what we heard."

My stomach knots as I remember Lila's suggestion to Ethan about my memories. "I promise I'm fine." But I'm not sure I am.

"Okay." She pulls me tighter against her and remains silent, leaving me to wonder what's going on in her head. I'm about to be daring and ask her, but then she says, "Man, I'm so going to date a drummer one day."

Okay, maybe I don't want to know what's going on in her head.

"You say that now, but next week it'll be the guy from Danny's Stop and Go," I tease. "Then it'll be the quarterback."

She peers over her shoulder at me, the florescent lighting reflecting in her green eyes. "Are you saying I'm flaky?" Her brow arches, challenging me.

"You do change your mind a lot."

"That's because there's too many opportunities roaming around in the world. It's hard to focus on just one." She rotates back around toward the stage and raises her voice as the drummer starts bashing on the symbols. "You know what we should do!" she shouts as the crowd goes wild. "We should join a band! There's these two guys from school, Nolan and Sage, who are looking for band members!"

"I'm not that great at the guitar yet!" I holler as I get bumped from every angle. *Breathe. Just breathe.* "And what about your issue with stage fright?"

"I'm going to conquer that fear one day!" She lifts her arms in the air and screams as the singer belts sultry lyrics through the microphone. "And you rock at the guitar! It's mad crazy how fast you caught on in just a month's time!"

"Ethan's a good teacher!" I shout, but my voice gets swallowed up by the screams, the singing, the bass, the entire scene of being a rock star.

Lyric gets lost in the rhythm, rocking and bobbing her head. Our bodies are perfectly aligned so every time she sways her hips, her ass rubs against my cock. The sensation is so intense that by the third song, I almost consider bailing.

But the way she moves.

Is breathtaking.

Consuming.

She owns me.

Makes me feel

so alive.

So petrified.

I can't breathe.

Dizzy.

Spinning out of control.

Reckless and wild.

I want.

Want. Want.

Something so

terrifying.

In the middle of my stream of thoughts, Lyric twirls around. Her eyes are large and glazed over, high on the music. I open my mouth to ask her what's up, but she glides her palms up my chest then wraps her arms around my neck. My muscles wind tight as she presses her breasts against me. Then, she stands on her tiptoes and places her lips against my ear.

"Strip me bare, peel me apart, layer by layer, steal my heart," she sings the lyrics of the song playing. Her voice is soft, not to her full potential, yet it's the most incredible sound that's ever graced my ears. I can only imagine what it would sound like if she *really* sang—striking enough to stop my heart probably. *"Let me stand naked in front of you, and pour my secrets out. Unravel me slowly, savoring each part."* She rolls her body against mine and her fingers trace the nape of my neck. *"Then let me do the same thing to you. Strip you apart."*

I start to move with her, even though I have no clue what I'm doing. No fucking idea. All I know is I'm left wanting, wanting, wanting.

Wanting her.

Wanting more.

But I'm too afraid to take it.

Chapter 7

Lyric

I'm a sporadic person. That's been a given since I first learned how to talk. So when I declare my love for someone, it shouldn't be that big of a surprise. Yet, it always seems to be with everyone. My parents especially. Whenever I proclaim my love for someone new, they seem shocked, like they half expected me to say someone else.

Ayden should know better by now, though, since he understands my little quirks better than anyone.

"I think I'm in love," I announce to him as I stroll into his bedroom.

He's situated on the bed, fiddling with the guitar Ethan bought him for his birthday a few months ago. After a little bit of practice, he's gotten pretty good at it, enough that he joined a band per my suggestion, and now he's living out my lifelong dream. But it's my own damn fault for letting my fear control me.

He glances up from his guitar as I shut the door, his fingers continuing to pluck the strings. "Who is it this time?

The drummer from that concert?" He seems more annoyed than usual.

Rolling up the paper I brought over with me, I narrow my eyes at him as I flop down onto the mattress on my stomach. "No, not him. And what do you mean 'this time'?" I prop up on my elbows as the sunlight hits my face through the window. "Are you mocking me, Ayden Gregory, about my frequency in love declarations?"

He rolls his eyes, lays the guitar aside on the mattress, and brushes strands of his black hair out of his eyes as he relaxes back on the bed. "This is the third time in the last four months you've barged into my room and said the exact same thing to me." I pout out my lip, and he sighs, gathering a guitar pick from the pillow. "Fine, who are you in love with?" He fiddles around with the pick, sketching the tip up and down the scars on the back of his hand.

I still don't know where the scars came from. I want to ask him, but any time I even mention Ayden's life before the Gregorys, he gets squeamish, which makes me question how he's going to handle the papers I brought over with me. I have to tell him, though. After spending the last few months searching for his siblings, I finally stumbled across something, not about his siblings, but about his past.

116

I kneel up on the bed in front of him. "It's William Stephington."

His face squishes in disgust. "Ew, that jock, steroid freak?"

"Hey." I swat his arm. "He's not a steroid freak."

"That's not what I heard." He frowns, staring at me undecidedly. "Lyric, I know you might not want to hear this, but I think you should stay away from that guy. And I really think you should talk to him for more than ten minutes before you decide you're in love with him."

"I've talked to him quite a few times at school. And besides, I agreed to go out with him tonight."

His frown deepens. "Lyric, the guy's got a reputation for being a ..." He deliberates his word choice while staring at a Pink Floyd poster on the ceiling that I gave him for his birthday. "A manwhore douche."

"Manwhore douche? Wow, those are some colorful words."

"Well, he is."

I scrape at my blue fingernail polish, choosing my next words carefully. "Even if he is, it doesn't matter, because I'm not a douche or a whore. I haven't even kissed a guy yet." I hop off the bed. "But that's going to change to-night."

He pulls a face, clearly irritated, which isn't typical for him. Usually, Ayden is the most agreeable person in the world, always trying to please everyone. "Don't waste your first kiss on that asshole."

"Hey, I've been saving my first kiss for over seventeen years now, so trust me when I say that when it happens, it's not going to be something I do with an asshole."

"He's not the guy who's going to change your soul, Lyric. Or make you write any better. He's not the life experience you're searching for."

I sternly point a finger at him. "Hey, I told you all that stuff in confidence."

His gaze scans the vacant room with his hands spread out. "Am I telling anyone else? No, I'm just reminding you what you told me—that this isn't what you want. You're saving your first kiss for a guy that will make you be able to pour your soul out onto paper, give you something to write about. And I don't believe that that's going to be William Stephington." His face twists with disgust again.

I fold my arms across my chest, and his gaze flicks to the papers in my hand. "Well, even if he isn't, maybe it's time to get this whole kissing thing over with. I mean, I'm seventeen years old, for God's sake. No one is a virgin kisser at that age. Jesus, Maggie kissed her first guy when she was like fourteen. I had my chance, too, but no, I had to hold on to this crazy idea that kisses were supposed to be all romantic and planned."

"It's not that bad of a concept."

"Yes it is. And it's time for me to grow up." I pause. "And why are you even lecturing me? I know you kissed a ton of girls before you came here."

It's just a guess, but when he doesn't deny it, I assume I'm right.

Grief engraves into his face. "Don't do that—change your dreams over some guy or belief based on other people. That's not the Lyric I know and love. Besides, you hardly even know the guy. You're way too trusting sometimes."

I sigh, because he's got me on that one. "Fine, I'll reconsider the kiss, but I'm still trusting him enough to go out on the date, because that's what I do." I back up for the door, knowing that's not true. I've passed up chance after chance of getting kissed, because my expectations are too high. "You know, if it really bothers you, you could always come with us."

"On your date with you?" he says dryly. "Yeah, that sounds like a lot of fun."

"No, to the party we're going to."

I know he won't. He made a commitment to do family movie night tonight, and Ayden hardly goes back on his commitments to the Gregorys, like he thinks he owes them for adopting him or something. Honestly, sometimes I believe that's exactly what he thinks, which is sad.

"I have band practice tonight." He drops the guitar pick onto the pillow and sits up, swinging his feet over the edge of the bed as he stretches his arms over his head. "And then movie night afterward."

I try not to stare when his shirt rides up, but it's always difficult. On top of having a beautiful face, Ayden's body is ridiculously amazing. Not super muscly or anything, just lean and toned.

One of my friends, Maggie, asked me how I can stand being friends with him without wanting to "get some of that." I tell her it's simple, because I don't look at him that way. Just as a friend. She looked at me as if I'd grown a third eye, which I had shrugged off. Yeah, Ayden is hot. That's a huge obvious given. And he's the best friend I could ever ask for. But I haven't felt the butterflies around him or the desire to kiss him. I haven't felt that with anyone yet. Maybe it's because I set the bar too high, but I'm contemplating lowering it tonight.

"So what." I sigh when Ayden finally adjusts his shirt back over his stomach. "Blow off movie night and come after practice is over. Sage and Nolan will probably be there anyway."

He pauses. "Where is it at?"

"Up at Maggie's house." I grip the doorknob, feeling upbeat at the idea that he might go. "Are you seriously considering going?"

He stands up and winds around his bed and over to me. "Yeah, maybe. If Sage and Nolan go there, I might catch a ride with them."

"Good." I have to stand up on my tiptoes to kiss him on the cheek. He flinches, like he always does whenever I touch him, but at least he allows me to. With almost anyone else, he freaks out. The only exception to this being Fiona, and sometimes Lila. "You need to do more fun things in your life, shy boy."

"No, I don't," he says in all seriousness. "I'm just going to keep an eye on you."

I ruffle his hair. "I don't need a babysitter."

"Yeah, you kind of do, and I have an endless list of reasons why. You think too much with your heart, Lyric, and not with your head."

"All right, I'll give you that." Shooting him one last conniving grin, I open the door and strut out of his room, calling over my shoulder, "See you tonight, babysitter."

I halt as I step over the threshold, realizing I still have the papers in my hand. "Oh, wait. There was actually a real reason why I came over here."

"You mean other than make another declaration of love," he jokes as I spin around.

"Yes, my friend." Sucking in a huge breath, I hand the papers over. "I found something out about you on the internet."

"About me?" The papers crinkle as he unrolls them.

"Yeah." I release a deafening breath, worried how this is going to go, but there was no way I could keep something like this from him. "It's about your tattoo."

He glances up from the papers, his grey eyes filled with terror. "I don't understand."

I move around to stand beside to him. "Well, I was

122

typing in random things that I thought might help us figure out stuff about your brother and sister. Then I started typing in homemade tattoos just to see what came up. After scrolling through an assload of images, I found this." I tap my finger against the paper. "I guess it's a pretty common thing to do—put tattoos on yourself. But the one you have belongs to some crazy group of people who believe the tattoo represents some kind of soul cleansing thing. I don't know. It sounds weird to me, but that's what all the articles say. And I guess they've done a lot of bad stuff, too."

He stares at the ink staining the paper in his hand. "Like what?"

"Like … kidnappings and things. You said a couple of months ago that you were taken by people with strange beliefs …" I trail off, hoping he'll explain more to me. I don't want to push him.

His fingers strangle the paper, the edges ruffling. "I wasn't necessarily taken … I was given away."

"By who?"

"My mother." His tone is sharp, his eyes cold, lost. He looks like a scared little boy.

My breath catches in my throat. "She gave you to those

people?"

"Left us with them," is all he says. He folds up the papers and chucks them on the desk. "I have a bunch of stuff to do before I head to practice."

I instantly regret showing him the paper, but there's not a whole lot that I can do about it now.

"All right, I'll see you later maybe."

He doesn't respond, so I leave the room, praying that I didn't break him.

Chapter 8

Lyric

I have about an hour until date time and should be getting ready, but instead I end up getting distracted with my notebook. A lot of the stuff coming out of me today is strange and mainly centered on my worry for Ayden, but since I still don't completely understand him or everything he went through, I feel as though my words are lacking. My lyrics usually do.

Honestly, I'm nowhere near where I want to be in any music area. I've yet to decide which instrument I want to focus on, haven't performed at all, and the idea of performing in front of anyone makes me want to hurl. It gets frustrating. Ayden, who barely talks to anyone, is perfectly fine standing up on stage and playing the guitar, while me, Miss Chatterbox, suffers from stage fright.

Go. Fucking. Figure.

About fifteen minutes before date time, I start the process of getting ready, moving slower than usual as I keep glancing out the window toward Ayden's bedroom. His curtain is shut, so I have no clue what he's doing.

Finally, after going through all of my clothes, I end up stealing a thin-strapped black dress from my mother's closet, and then slip a leather jacket on since it's fall and sometimes the nights can sometimes get a little breezy. I dab on some kohl eyeliner and pink lip gloss, then top off the look with my favorite pair of boots before I go downstairs to wait for my date.

I find my dad lounging on the living room sofa, jotting down lyrics in his own notebook. He glances up when I enter.

"Where are you headed to all dressed up?" he asks, setting the pen and notebook down on the sofa cushion beside him.

"To a party." I drop down in the chair across from him and kick my feet up on an antique trunk that acts as a coffee table.

He puts on his interrogation face. "And where is this party?"

"At Maggie's house." I check my watch. "Mom already went over this with me, Dad."

"And who are you going with?" he continues, ignoring my last statement.

126

"With a guy from school."

"Which one?"

"Someone you haven't met yet." I lower my feet to the floor. "His name's William Stephington."

"And what does this William do?" he asks, reaching for his soda that's on the trunk.

"He goes to school with me." I fiddle with one of the leather bands on my wrists. "He's on the football team, too."

His grip constricts on the soda can as he frowns. "Football? Really?"

"What? There's nothing wrong with football guys."

"Yeah, but ... it just doesn't seem like your type."

"I don't even know my type yet." I resist an eye roll. Jesus, he's getting weirder and weirder about guys the more I go out on dates.

He places the can back on the trunk then rests his arms on his knees. "Is Ayden going to this party?"

I shrug, feeling a lump swell in my throat as I remember the coldness in his eyes when I left his room. "I invited him, and he seemed like he might show up, but with Ayden you can never be sure. He might end up feeling too guilty about missing movie night."

Maybe I should go check on him before I leave?

Or at least text him.

I just need to know that he's okay.

My dad ponders over something then sticks his hand into the pocket of his jeans. "I'm going to call Ethan to see if I can find out." He presses a button then puts the phone to his ear while I retrieve my cell from my jacket pocket to text Ayden.

"Yeah, you do that." I jump to my feet when I hear a horn honk outside. "That's my ride. Have fun with your phone call." I scurry for the door with the phone clutched in my hand.

"Lyric Scott, get your butt back here."

Dammit, so close.

I spin around and smile innocently at him. "Yes, Daddy."

"Don't you 'yes Daddy' me." He nods his head toward the window at the driveway where the engine of William's car is rumbling. "I have to meet him before you get in that car with him."

My shoulders slacken. "What, you don't trust my judgment?"

He dithers with indecision. "No, not really. You are my daughter after all."

I blow out a frustrated breath. "Fine. You can walk me to the car and meet him." I aim a finger at him. "But don't be weirdo, strict dad."

He rolls his eyes as he stuffs his phone back inside his pocket. "Lyric, when it comes to you dating guys, I will always be weirdo, strict dad, but only because I love you."

Sighing, I lead him out to William, knowing my dad's already docking points for the Mercedes he's driving. William appears wigged out when I stroll up to the driver's side and rap on the glass.

He rolls the window down. "What's up?" He casts a glimpse over my shoulder at my dad. His appearance is going to be strike two—blonde hair slicked back, a polo shirt, and his somewhat cocky grin isn't going to impress him.

"William, this is my dad." I motion back and forth between them. "Dad, this is William."

My dad eyeballs the sleek lines of the car with his face screwed up tight, like he just tasted something bitter. "How long have you had your license?"

"For about a year." William flicks a *what the hell* look

at me.

Things only continue to go downhill as my dad fires question after question at him. By the time we're pulling out of the driveway, fifteen minutes have passed since I first walked out of the house.

"Sorry about that," I say as I buckle my seatbelt. "I'm not sure what got into him today."

William squirms in his seat as he adjusts the mirror. "No worries. I just didn't expect *your* dad to be so uptight."

"What do you mean by *your* dad?"

He shrugs as he shifts gears and speeds up. "I just figured with as laid back as you are that your parents would be pretty chill."

I feel a little bit defensive, which is really out of character for me. Usually I try to stay all peace, love, and sunshine. "He was just making sure his daughter wasn't driving off with a psychopath."

He laughs, kind of snidely. "He seemed a little overly intense, if you ask me."

Okay, maybe Ayden was right. Perhaps I should spend more time with a guy before I proclaim that I'm in love with him.

"Sorry," he quickly says when he catches sight of my

disappointment. "I just don't do well with parents." He reaches across the console and wraps his fingers around my bare knee. "Let's drop it, though, and have some fun tonight." He flashes me his infamous dimpled grin.

I smile back, but I'm suddenly not feeling him.

As William starts rambling about sports, I slide my finger across the screen of my phone and send Ayden a text.

Me: Hey, so I just wanted to see if u were ok. U looked super upset when I left and I feel like maybe I might have pushed u a little too far... If u need to talk or want to meet up later, I'm totally down for it. William might be a bust anyway.

I slide my phone into my pocket, waiting for a reply. By the time we arrive at the party, I'm still feeling super down and a bit anxious, so when William offers me a drink, I take it, even though I've tried to avoid alcohol since the whole scotch incident.

William flashes me his pearly whites as I guzzle down half the cup in one gulp. "Hell yeah!" he cheers over the pop music I loathe, blasting so loudly I can feel the bass in my chest.

I lick a drop of the spiked punch off the bottom of my lip, slightly more at ease as the alcohol settles into my system. "Want to dance!" I shout, figuring anything will be better than talking about sports some more.

Without waiting for him to respond, I hand him my drink, wiggle out of my jacket and shake my ass toward the dance floor, twirling around and around.

I waggle my fingers at my friend Maggie, who's dancing in the corner with a guy that looks old enough to be in college. She winks at me and wiggles her eyebrows suggestively right as someone places their hands on my waist.

"You dance fucking amazing," William whispers in my ear, his breath hot on my skin and reeking of Bacardi.

I smile at myself then whirl around and really show him what dancing is, rocking and grinding my hips against his. He moves with me, rubbing against me as his hands travel all over my body, gripping at my flesh.

"God, you smell so fucking good." His teeth graze my neck as his hand cups my ass.

The music suddenly screams at my eardrums to the point where I can't stand it anymore.

I'm so not ready for this tonight.

I tense and push back, putting room between our bodies. "Maybe we should slow things down just a bit."

He seems a little pissed, but calms down and says, "How about we go out back where it's a little bit quieter and talk. There are people out there, too, so we won't be alone."

I nod, relieved that he's not being pushy about my stiffness. That's pretty much the only thing he's done right the entire night, so I take it.

He pours us both another drink in the kitchen area before he slips his fingers through mine and steers me through Maggie's house. I've never actually been to her home before, not her father's house anyway. William seems to know his way around as he maneuvers through the throng of people drinking, dancing, laughing, and playing pool. Some I go to high school with, while others look old enough to be in college.

"This house is huge!" I yell over the music as we veer down a narrow hallway lined with shut doors. The lighting is dim, the music softer.

He peers over his shoulder. "Drink up," he says, nodding at the cup in my hand. His expression is darker than it was minutes ago. Oddly enough, he seems extremely relaxed. It makes me hesitate. Red flags go up.

All of a sudden, he's tugging me into a dark room with a bed and a dresser. He doesn't turn the lights on as he closes and locks the door behind us. A little too late, I painfully realize that Ayden might have been right about William. And myself, too. I do think with my heart too much. Do trust people too much.

And now I've walked head-on into trouble.

Chapter 9

Ayden

I hate parties. Growing up in the midst of them gave me an ugly outlook on what can come from too much partying. My mother was a hardcore partier. Her drug of choice was everything and anything she could get her hands on. It aged her quickly and turned her into a nasty person, one who was incapable of loving and did the most awful things to people, including her own children. And that's how she died, a doped-up druggie who hated the world and left scars on her offspring. It was a sad, pathetic waste of a life. At her funeral, I vowed that I would never turn into her.

I almost did, though, as I got lost in the system, getting bitter with each home I was passed through. But then I lucked out and ended up with the Gregorys, who showed me that people could love one another unconditionally and gave me hope that maybe trusting people was a possibility. That perhaps even love was a possibility. That's what my therapist is trying to convince me.

Jessica Sorensen

"You're too afraid to feel all the horrible emotions you shut down as a child." He told me that today while I sat in his office, fidgety as usual. You would think after nine months of monthly visits with him I would be more relaxed, yet I never am. "That fear is blocking out all of the good emotions as well as some of your memories."

I hadn't responded.

Part of me agrees with him, but I am doing better with dealing my emotions, not shutting down so much and keeping my feelings to myself. Then I saw that damn paper and was reminded of stuff forgotten. I snapped at Lyric, which is gnawing at me more than anything.

"Ayden, tell Kale to stop teasing me!" Fiona shouts from the kitchen table as Kale throws a pencil at her.

I tear my attention from my thoughts and the cookie I've been nibbling on for the last ten minutes.

Fiona is probably the most spoiled by all of us. I once heard Lila and Ethan talking about how they ended up adopting her. She was born by a mother who was doped-up on heroin. She had a lot of health problems because of this, so no one wanted to adopt her. Like me, she was passed through many homes until she ended up here four years ago. Other than the fact that she's a bit small for her age, she seems normal. Spunky even.

All have their own stories, though.

Everyone does when you really think about it.

It's something I've learned while I've been here. That I'm not as alone as I once thought.

"Kale, leave her alone," I say as I dig a soda out of the fridge.

Kale's shoulders slump as he sets the pencils down on the table. "Whatever." He sulks out of the kitchen.

Fiona flips him the bird then she smiles sweetly at me. "Thank you, Ayden. You're the best brother ever."

I pop the tab on the can, feeling the slightest bit of guilt churn in my gut as I think of my brother and sister, and the paper Lyric showed me with the tattoo on it.

"What are you working on?" I change the subject as I peek at her drawing. It's of a butterfly—most of them are. "That's actually really good." It's the truth, too. The girl is damn talented at drawing. Equally as good as Lyric and her mother, which says a lot.

"I know. I just wish I could get the butterfly out of my head and draw something else." She sits down and plucks up the pencil. "I can never seem to stop thinking about them. It's like a dream stuck in my head."

My brows furrow. "Is it something from your child-hood maybe?"

"Could be." That's all she gives me, and I will never, *ever* press her to tell me more when it's clear she doesn't want to. "Do you think I'll be able to be an artist one day?"

"I think you can be whatever you want," I repeat the words Lila keeps saying to Kale when he asks her a similar question about being a comic book artist. "As long as you work hard."

Fiona works on shading in the wings while humming a song under her breath. "Do you think Mrs. Scott would give me art lessons? She's super good at painting and stuff. And I want to learn to do that. I mean, I like drawing, but I think it's time for an upgrade."

"You could always ask her," I say, trying not to think about Lyric going out with that douche tonight, yet it creeps into my mind and leaves a foul feeling in the pit of my stomach, almost as heavy as when I saw that paper she handed me.

This William asshole has a reputation for treating girls like shit. It's guys like him that will burn Lyric's feisty, trusting, carefree inner fire right out of her. And while that fire has gotten me in trouble quite a few times, I never, *ever* want it to burn out. It's what got me breathing again, brought me back to life, keeps me breathing. As selfish as it makes me sound, I want Lyric all to myself. I just wish I could give her a little of what she gives me back, instead of freaking out on her all the time.

I sneak up to my bedroom and jot some of my thoughts about Lyric into a notebook. It's something I started doing six months ago when my therapist suggested I find a way to clear out my head. I think that he was aiming more along the lines of a journal, but the pages are filled with song lyrics than my inner thoughts and desires.

Tucking the notebook back into the dresser drawer, I grab my guitar and jog down the stairs. Lila is filling up a pot under the faucet when I enter the kitchen, and fresh vegetables and seasonings cover the counters. She's obviously planning a big meal, so now I feel guilt-ridden about going to the party.

"I'm going to band practice," I tell her as she shuts the water off. "It's still okay if I take the car, right?" I've been a little offish since I overheard the conversation between her and Ethan. I'm not sure why, but it feels like they're keeping something from me about myself or my brother and sister.

"Do you know what time you're going to be back? I want to make sure I have dessert ready and everyone settled down for movie time."

"About that ..." I shift my guitar case into my other hand. "I was kind of wondering if maybe I could go to a party after band practice."

She carries the pan full of water to the stove. "Is it the one Lyric went to with that William guy?"

"How did you know about that?"

"Micha mentioned something about it just a few minutes ago." She switches the heat up on the stove. "He wanted to know if you were going. I think he's not handling this whole Lyric dating thing very well and wanted you to check up on her."

"So, is it okay if I go?" I ask, opening the fridge to grab another soda. "I mean, I can come home if you want me to. In fact, maybe I should. I promised you guys a movie night."

She sighs as she rounds the counter toward me. "Ayden, you don't need to please us all the time." She circles her arms around me as I'm pushing the fridge door shut.

"Go to the party."

I hold my breath and awkwardly pat her back, my grip on the soda can nearly crushing the metal. "Are you sure?"

"Yes." She pulls back, retrieves the car keys from her pocket, and drops them into my palm. "Just do me a favor. When you get there, check on Lyric, and then text me so Micha will stop sending me texts."

"Okay, that I can do." I enfold my fingers around the keys. "But can I ask you one more thing?"

"Of course, sweetie. You can ask me anything. You know that."

I wasn't planning on asking her today, but after the tattoo thing brought up unwanted memories, I need to know for my own sanity. "I was just wondering if you found anything out about my brother yet? I know you said we'd check back when he was eighteen, and now he is, so ..." I clutch the handle of my guitar case as her skin pales.

"Oh, Ayden." She embraces me so tightly the air gets ripped from my lungs. "I'm sorry ... I've been meaning to tell you, but I just couldn't figure out how. I guess he ran away from the last foster home he was at, which was over a year ago. No one's seen or heard from him since."

My fingers ball into fists, the sharp edges of the keys slicing into my skin. I want to grasp onto her. Cry. But I can't do that—can't let go in that kind of way—so I pull back.

"Okay, thanks for trying." I start for the door, trying not to hyperventilate.

"Ayden, are you going to be okay?" she calls after me.

"Not really." The truth slips from my lips, but before she can utter anything else, I'm out the door.

***

Two hours later, I'm feeling a tad bit better. Playing always does that for me. It helped me to stop thinking of my brother and worrying about Lyric. Lyric also text me, saying she wants to meet up and wasn't feeling William, which made me twistedly happy inside. I had text her back, replying okay, but she still hasn't responded. That's Lyric, though. She's probably gotten sidetracked by someone.

Sage and Nolan are in the car with me as we roll up to the house in Lila's BMW. The fancy car blends in with the rest of others parked around the house. No surprise, since the house is a freaking mansion. I mean, the home I live in is pretty fucking big, but this damn thing looks like it has three stories and a basement. I'm never going to find Lyric here.

I've already sent her multiple texts by the time I enter the home, but she still hasn't responded. As soon as I step foot into the foyer, I discover why. The music is blaring so loud the floors and windows are vibrating.

"Dude, this music sucks balls!" Sage yells over the noise, pulling a repulsed face at a machine pouring fog across the dance area, like we're in a freaking club or something. He rakes his hand through his hair. "I need a fucking drink."

As he vanishes into the crowd and the smog, Nolan stuffs his hands into his pockets. "I'm going to go find Anna. Are you going to be okay?"

"I can take care of myself, man," I say, even though the amount of people crammed into the room is making me feel as if the walls are closing in. This is the last thing I needed tonight after finding out Lila couldn't find anything out about my brother.

I need to find Lyric and get the hell out of here.

"But I know how you get in crowds!" Nolan has to yell in order for me to hear him over the song. "And around people!"

I wave him off. "I'll be fine. Go get some."

He grins then the crowd swallows him up as he dives into the insanity.

I start my search for Lyric, pushing my way through sweaty, intoxicated people, until I manage to find the enormous kitchen that could easily be as big as the entire top floor of my house. I ask if anyone has seen her, but since I usually don't speak until I have to, it's apparent that's made the people I go to school with skittish around me.

Finally, I stumble across Maggie. She's near the dance area with a cup in her hand, her attention fixed on a short, stocky guy that looks like he's in college.

I squeeze past people, moving in her direction across the room. Everyone is dancing, and I get rubbed up on more than once. Add the smoke in the air, and I feel like I'm going to suffocate to death. I still keep going, though, telling myself to suck it up. That this isn't the past. Just a party. Nothing more. But images of my brother and I chained to that damn wall creep up and stab me in the brain. It feels like my skull is bleeding. All I want to do is find a place to curl up and cry.

He disappeared without a trace.

Gone to who knows where.

Lost in a sea of people.

Who will never understand.

Maybe he isn't just lost, though.

Fuck, what if he's dead?

"Hey, have you seen Lyric?" I ask when I manage to get beside Maggie, one of the few people who aren't afraid of me.

Her drunken gaze lights up as she scans me over from head to toe. "Hey, sexy. I feel so special. You never come to parties."

The stocky guy she's with gives me a nasty look, like I'm trying to cramp his style. But one good thing about my intimidation factor is when I retaliate with a dirty look, he backs off.

"I thought I'd come and see what this whole thing was about," I lie. "But I need to find Lyric and check in on her. I promised I would."

"You are so good to her. I wish I had someone like you for myself." She trails her fingers up and down my stomach then flattens her palm against my chest.

As memories prickle at the back of my mind, I almost

shove her.

Breathe, just breathe.

Breathe, breathe, breathe.

Into the light, out of the dark.

To the life with Lyric.

Where no one can touch you.

Break you apart.

Where you don't have to see or feel.

What was done to you.

What destroyed you.

I inch out of her reach, and her hand remains suspended in the air as her brows dip.

"Look, I really need to find Lyric," I tell her, stuffing my hands into my pockets to keep from pushing her away.

Her face bunches up as she frowns. "The last time I saw her, she was heading into one of the bedrooms with William."

My heart hammers inside my chest, my eardrums ringing louder than the song. "Where is this bedroom?" My voice comes out sharper than I mean to, but seriously, what the hell is Lyric thinking going into a bedroom with William Stephington?

Maggie points her finger toward the back of the house.

"It's back there, down the hallway." She swigs a mouthful from the cup in her hand. "God, Ayden, you need to chillax. She can go back to a room with a guy without your permission."

I scowl at her then start shoving through the crowd, roughly pushing people out of my way. It takes me a few minutes to get to the hallway Maggie pointed to, but I manage. The first door I open is a closet. The next is a bedroom, but it's empty, so I try the next one. And the next. All are vacant, except for the last one, which has a couple occupying it. They're going at it like rabbits, and I get an eyeful before I get the door shut.

What the hell am I doing? If Lyric is back here doing something with William, then what? I'm going to walk in and tell her to stop? Then she would get pissed off at me, and honestly, I don't think I could handle seeing her doing that with a guy.

Giving up on the bedrooms, I spin back around and make a path for the kitchen again. Halfway down the hall, my phone vibrates from inside my pocket. I pause to fish it out and exhale a breath of relief when I see the text is from Lyric.

Lyric: U didn't by chance come to the party, did u?

Me: Yeah, I'm here right now. Where r u?

Lyric: In the bathroom.

Me: Okay, meet me in the kitchen when u come out.

Lyric: I can't.

Me: Can't what? Meet me in the kitchen?

Lyric: No, come out of the bathroom.

Me: R u sick?

Lyric: No.

Me: Then what's wrong?

When she doesn't respond, I grow anxious.

Me: R u hurt?

Lyric: Kind of.

Me: Lyric, where the fuck r u?

Lyric: I'm in the bathroom on the second floor near the start of the hallway. But, Ayden, u don't need to come up here. I'm fine.

Like hell I don't.

I knock people out of the way as I storm back through the kitchen and toward the massive spiral stairway that coils to the second floor. Different scenarios play in my head as my mind goes wild, trying to figure out what happened. With Lyric, it's hard to say. The girl is a freaking daredevil, but for some reason, I'm betting this has to do with William.

The top of the stairs is much quieter and less populated. Only a group of seven or eight are lurking around, drinking and smoking, including Sage.

"Hey, do you know where the bathroom is?" I ask him as he takes a deep hit from a joint.

He coughs smoke in my face as he exhales, passing the rolled up paper to the next guy. "Sorry, about that," he says as I fan my hand in front of my face. "Yeah, it's the fifth door down, but I wouldn't bother. Some chick's been locked in there for like an hour."

I'm off before he can even finish his sentence, rushing past doors. When I reach the fifth one, it's locked, so I bang my fist against the heavy wood.

"Lyric, open the door. It's me."

A beat goes by before I hear the lock click. I push the door open and step into the dark, narrow room. Moonlight trickles in from the window above the bathtub, highlighting Lyric's silhouette.

"Why the hell do you have the light off?" I feel around on the wall until my fingers brush against the switch. I flip it on, blinking against the bright light.

"You were right," Lyric says, only her voice sounds so wrong, like it's excruciating to speak, which might be because she has a swollen lip. "I'm way too trusting for my own good."

My lips part in shock at the sight of her. Her cheeks are enflamed and one of the straps of her dress is missing, as if someone ripped it off. The front has fallen down, too, so I can see the top of her bra. Her blond hair is tangled around her pained face and mascara and tears stain her cheeks.

She cups her hand to her cheek. "God, my face fucking hurts."

That yanks me out of my trance.

"What the hell did he do to you?" I pause when her fingers drift to the hem of her dress.

God, no. Please don't let it be that. I don't know if I can handle that. It'll be too much, and I need to be able to handle this for her.

"Did he …?" I can't even say it aloud, as I'm pulled away to a different time, place, life that binds me at the wrists and slices my flesh open.

I don't want to remember it.

Please.

Don't let me remember it.

Right now.

Ever.

She shakes her head, hugging her arms around herself. "No, he didn't get that far."

My breathing comes out ragged as I battle to stay calm. "Where is he?"

She shrugs. "I don't know. Probably icing his balls."

I cock my head to the side. "Huh?"

"Well, I did kick him there enough times that he probably won't be able to have children anymore," she says matter-of-factly, her eyes lacking so much emotion it kills me to look at them.

I miss her fire. Her life.

He better not have stolen that away from her.

Taken *anything* away from her.

I pierce my nails into the flesh of my palms. "How did you get the fat lip and the welt on your cheek?"

She lowers herself onto the shut toilet then drops her head into her hands. "I thought we were going outside and realized too late he was taking me to a bedroom. When we got in there, he locked the door and shoved me down on the bed. I hit my face on the headboard and bit my lip."

I cautiously inch past the sink toward her. "What about your dress? How did it ... get torn?"

Her breathing quickens and her bottom lip quivers. "I said he didn't rape me, but that doesn't mean he didn't try." She drags her fingers down her face as she stares helplessly at me. "God, I'm so stupid. You were right. I do think too much with my heart."

Something snaps inside me. Breaks. Shatters. I'm not sure if it's because she doubts her heart, or that he tried to rape her. Whatever it is, I can't stop the thoughts from emerging.

House of locks. Walls of metal.

Searing pain. Scorching into me.

Branded forever, like bleeding ink.

I suck in an uneven breath.

William is going to fucking pay for what he did.

"I'll be right back." My voice is low and controlled, despite the fact that I feel more out of control than I ever have. I reel around and yank the door open.

"No, Ayden, don't," Lyric begs, hopping up from the toilet and chasing after me.

But I storm out the door, slamming it behind me with

only a single thought in my mind.

Make William pay.

Protect Lyric.

Like no one ever did for me.

I find the douche bag in the kitchen, near the drink section, chatting with some girl from our school, standing a bit awkwardly as he throws back a shot.

Of course he'd be with a fucking girl.

He spots me when I'm about two steps away from him, and by the way the color drains from his face, I can tell he knows why I'm here, and he's afraid. He fucking should be. I had been good at refraining from violence for a while, but I'm making an exception right now for Lyric.

I don't even slow down as I reach him, my feet keeping momentum as I crane my arm back. He starts to stagger back into the counter, but not quick enough, and I bash my knuckles straight into his nose. There's a crack then blood streams from his nostrils, and then he crumples to the floor. The crowd creates a gap as people skitter away from the scene, some cursing, and a few girls even start crying.

"You're going to fucking pay for that," he growls as he rolls onto his back, cupping his bloody nose.

I crouch down beside him, and his eyes widen and fill with fear. "If you ever so much as look at Lyric again, I will put you in the hospital. You got it?"

He shakes his head, cursing as blood drips down the back of his hands. "I'm going to sue your ass for this."

I lean down in his face. "Do. You. Get. What. I'm. Saying?"

Scowling, he nods. It takes every amount of my strength to stand up without punching him in the face again.

By the time I reach the stairway, my fists are trembling and blood is staining my knuckles and scars. I start to hyperventilate. I try to force the images back, but the flashbacks are too intense this time and emotions overwhelm me.

Claws.

Blood.

The walls are closing in.

They tell me this is how life is supposed to be.

For me to be trapped.

Confined.

A prisoner in a home filled with madness.

That my mother stuck me in.

Gave me up.

Just like that.

As if I was a stray dog she didn't want.

I can almost feel the metal biting at my wrists, and all I can do is grip onto the railing, and pray they'll be over soon.

That I'll forget again.

Chapter 10

Lyric

This is one of the worst nights of my life. I'm lucky, though. It could have gone a lot worse. William could have gotten what he was trying to steal. He got as far as kissing me and reaching under my dress before I managed to knee the crap out of his balls. Then he collapsed to the floor, and I ran out of the room.

But the damn idiot stole my first kiss!

That I can never get back.

And now Ayden has gone after him to do God knows what. I've never seen him that pissed off before. It has me extremely worried.

I'd been hiding out in the bathroom, embarrassed about how I looked, like everyone would be able to tell what happened by my appearance.

After sending Ayden countless texts, I give up and crack the door open, peering into the hallway. I spot Sage, his bright blue hair making him stand out like a bluebird in a sea of crows. He definitely has his own unique style. Tall and lean, he wears a lot of different shades of clothing, yet all of them are dark with murky tones. He has countless piercings, including three in his brow and one in his tongue.

He's chatting with his buddies, so I open the door all the way and stick my head out.

"Sage," I hiss, waving him over.

When he glances at me, his brows knit as he strides over. He has a joint in his hand and reeks of pot, but Sage is known as the school pothead, so it's no surprise. He can play the drums like a boss, though, so he's cool in my book.

"What's up?" His blue-eyed gaze scans me. "Holy shit. Are you okay, Lyric?"

"I'm fine. But can you go find Ayden? I think he might be in some trouble."

"Yeah, I saw him storming down the hall, looking like he was about to murder someone."

I bite down on my lip, instantly regretting it when pain sears across my face. "I'm kind of worried that he might try exactly that."

He positions the joint between his lips. "I'm on it."

I shut the door as he strides toward the stairs. Then, I

sink to the floor and very impatiently wait for Sage to either come back, or hopefully Ayden to return. Seconds tick by. Minutes. Right in the midst of deciding to go out myself, the door finally swings open.

"Oh, thank God." I sigh in relief as Ayden trudges into the bathroom. My gaze immediately drops to his hand cradled at his side, and I jump to my feet. "Why is there blood all over your knuckles?" I grab his hand and jerk it toward me. When his face contorts in pain, I loosen my hold.

"I haven't hit someone since I was fourteen," he mutters, stretching out the fingers of his uninjured hand. "I forgot that I wasn't supposed to use my knuckles."

I gently wipe some of the blood off his skin, surprised he doesn't stop me when my fingertips graze his scars. "But whose blood is this? Because I don't see any fresh cuts."

His gaze bores into me. "Whose do you think it is, Lyric?"

My heart beats wildly inside my chest. "You didn't have to hit him. I kicked him plenty of times."

"Yeah, I did. He *hurt* you." An uneven breath slips from his lips. "I should have done worse to him."

I tell myself to breathe, but my lungs can't seem to

figure out how to get the oxygen they need. "But it was kind of my fault. I mean, I had a bad feeling the moment I got into the car with him, but like you said, I don't always think with my head, and I trust people too much."

"Hey." He delicately cups my wounded cheek, his fingers splaying across my flesh. "Bad decision or not, none of this was your fault. He can't put his hands on you just because he's stronger than you. He had no right to touch you." His throat muscles move as he swallows hard then he promptly removes his hand from my face. "No one does unless you want them to."

I'm suddenly hyperaware of how long his eyelashes are and how perfectly kissable his lips look. When did he get so beautiful? I mean, he was always beautiful, but never *this* beautiful.

I rapidly shove the thought from my mind. *Jesus, Lyric, what the hell is wrong with you? Totally inappropriate.*

"Thank you, Ayden." I throw my arms around his neck and latch onto him. "You're the best friend I could ever ask for. No, you're more than that. Way, way more than that."

For the first time ever, he hugs me back. Honestly, it's kind of an awkward hug, because he keeps moving his hands around, unsure where to put them, until finally he decides to circle his arms around my waist.

As his warmth encompasses me, I inhale with a faint smile on my lips. I can almost feel it, the potential for a song surfacing in the back of my mind. Not about this night. Not about William. No, oddly enough it's about this hug.

"We should get you home," he whispers in my hair.

I pull back to look at him. "I don't want anyone seeing me like this." I glance down at the torn strap of my dress and the top of my bra sticking out. "And I lost my jacket, so I can't even cover up."

"We can fix that." He shucks his hoodie off and holds it out for me to put on. After I slide my arms in the sleeves, he snatches up one of the hand towels, gets it wet underneath the faucet, and begins carefully cleaning the smeared makeup from my face as I sit down on the counter, letting my legs dangle over the edge.

I watch him as he works, his intense gaze fixated on what he's doing. I notice the slightest quiver in his fingers and wonder what's causing it. If he's afraid, worried, angry, what? With Ayden, it's always complicated, like trying to figure out a story in a closed book.

"There." He moves back from me and tosses the towel into the sink. "That should be good enough to get you out of here without too many questions."

I twist around and peer at my reflection in the mirror. Besides the welt and cut lip, my face is seamlessly clean, as if tonight never happened. As if it was erased.

At least on the outside.

On the inside, the night scorches vividly inside my mind.

Tears begin to sting at my eyes again as the shock wears off.

Ayden tangles his fingers with mine and helps me down from the counter. "Come on, let's get you out of here." He steers us out the door, saying something to Sage before we start toward the bottom floor.

I stay close to him, clinging to his hand, with my face pressed against the back of his shirt that smells like his cologne. I focus on his scent as we make our way through the house, counting each step, each racing beat of my heart, each unstable breath.

I only feel safe again when I'm in the passenger seat of Lila's car and Ayden is driving down the road, away from that house, away from the party, away from William and this night.

"I'm going to think with my head more from now on." I rest my swollen cheek against the cool window. "And not trust people so damn much."

"Lyric, that's not what I meant when I said that." He turns down the stereo's volume, so the only noise filling the cab is the humming of the engine and the softness of our breathing. "I love that you don't always think with your head. It makes life interesting and keeps me from going crazy. And if it wouldn't have been for you being so damn trusting toward me, I would have … well, life would have been a lot harder."

I rotate my head toward him. "Really? You even feel this way when it gets you into trouble? Like fights. And crashing bikes. Drinking."

His jaw clenches. "It's not the first fight I've been in, or the first time I've drank."

William's blood still stains his knuckles and his scars. I've never flat out asked him where he got the scars from, and quite honestly, I'm afraid to after what happened with the tattoo thing earlier—afraid I'll scare him off again—so I opt for a different route.

"What kind of fights did you get into?" I watch him through the darkness with my knees pulled up, my head resting against the leather of the seat.

When he smashes his lips together, I figure he's going to remain silent and shut down like he normally does, but then his lips part.

"When I was fourteen, this guy from school came after me with a knife because he thought I hooked up with his girlfriend," he starts, staring out at the winding road ahead of us. "I clocked him in the face before he could cut me, but ended up splitting my knuckles open."

I hesitate before I ask, "Is that where the scars on your hand came from?"

His knuckles whiten as he grips the steering wheel. "No, someone else did that to me ... the same people who put the tattoo on me." His grip tightens even more. "I don't even remember what was done to me, though, so it doesn't matter."

It does matter, though.

Everything about him matters.

His voice is colder than I've ever heard it, so I drop the subject, not wanting to push him any further tonight.

"I can't believe a guy tried to stab you when you were fourteen." I trace circles on the console, wondering what it must have been like for him. "I barely used curse words when I was that old."

He gives me a sidelong glance. "You've had a good life. You shouldn't be sad about it. I know that you wish your life was more complicated so you could write better, but trust me, it's not worth the sacrifice."

"I'm not sad right now because of that." I face forward in my seat and wrap my arms around myself. "I'm sad because you haven't always had a good life; you deserve to have the best."

A beat of silence goes by.

"Life is getting ... easier for me."

Before I can say anything else, he cranks up the radio again.

We don't speak for the rest of the drive home. I rack my brain for a way to make him feel better. But by the time we're pulling up to our houses, I still have no clue what to do or say.

All the lights are off at my house so I have some time to think about what I'm going to tell my mom and dad about tonight without them losing their shit.

"You want me to come up and hang out with you until they get home?" Ayden asks, parking in front of his garage and silencing the engine.

I nod then unfasten my seatbelt and drag my butt out of the car.

While we're heading up to my bedroom, I text my parents to find out where they are. Turns out, my mother had to work late and my dad went down to the gallery to spend time with her. The two of them are so adorable that it makes me sick. And envious. I know their story. They grew up together. Were best friends who fell in love. They wrote songs about each other, and painted portraits of their undying love. Usually this makes me smile, but tonight, gag me. Seriously. I feel so bitter.

"I just want to go to bed and forget this night ever happened." I kick the bedroom door open and wrestle the hoodie off. "I should probably take a shower first."

Ayden clicks on the lamp, sits down on my bed, and collects my iPod from my cluttered nightstand. "I'll chill out on your bed and go through your song collection, preparing for your next music quiz." A small trace of a smile graces his lips.

Relief sweeps through me like a gentle breeze. *Maybe I didn't break him after all.*

After I grab some clothes from the dresser, I duck into the bathroom and take a quick shower, scrubbing my skin until it's raw and red, trying to cleanse the icky feeling off. I know tonight could have been a lot worse, but what happened still makes me feel sick to my stomach. Everything aches and my heart feels so dark. I hate the feeling. I want my sunshine back.

Tears spill from my eyes as I sink down into the bathtub and hug my knees to my chest. By the time I return to my bedroom, I'm exhausted, my eyes are puffy, my face hurts, and I'm ready to go to sleep.

Ayden is still in my bed like he said he would be, stretched out on the mattress with his back resting against the headboard. He has my ear buds in, and he's bobbing his head to the music as he thrums his fingers against his knee.

I collapse face first beside him and he quickly tugs on the cord, pulling out one of the earbuds. "Feeling any better?"

I bury my face into the pillow. "Kind of. I just want to go to sleep."

He lies down and rotates on his side, facing me. "Then

go to sleep. I'll stay with you until your mom and dad get home."

I close my eyes. "I feel so icky."

There's a pause then he lightly places his hand on my back. My eyelids flutter open at the contact of his warm fingertips. He's so close that his warm breath dusts my cheeks.

"You shouldn't feel icky," he says softly, his hand starting to massage the throbbing muscles of my back. "You did nothing wrong, but trust people too much. That's never a bad thing. Don't ever lose that."

"I'll try, but ..." I sink deeper into the pillow as tears sting my eyes again. "But he stuck his tongue down my throat, and it was the most disgusting kiss ever. I rinsed and brushed my teeth, but I swear to God, I can still feel it on me."

When he grows silent again, I crack an eyelid open. He's dazing off over my shoulder with undiluted pain in his eyes. The realness of him causes my heart to stutter, and my fingers yearn to jot down unwritten words.

God, what has he been through to create such a look?

When his focus lands back on me, his eyes burn fiercely, as if he's terrified out of his damn mind "Shut your eyes," he whispers, almost horrified.

I do as he says without question, trusting him completely, even though his intensity is enough to make the calmest person in the world feel disconcerted.

He sticks the earbud in my ear and the gloomy, unhurried beat of Radiohead's "How To Disappear Completely" soaks through my wounded soul.

"You picked the perfect song," I mutter as the music engulfs me. "This is exactly what I—"

His lips brush mine, stealing the words right from my mouth. My breath catches in my throat. My first instinct is to pull away, but I don't want to. I want to stay. Let him erase that last few hours from my mind.

I keep my eyes shut, too afraid to open them as his lips timidly start to move against mine. Just a whisper of a graze. A heart-stopping brush. A soul-drowning taste. He does it again and again, taking his time, erasing all the ickiness from tonight.

As I absorb each soft graze, his tongue slowly follows, slipping into my mouth. I gasp, but still don't open my eyes. I barely move. Can hardly think. And when he pulls back, gently biting at my bottom lip, I stop breathing all together.

That burn songs promise.

Blazes in me.

Hot and scorching.

So sweltering and mind-numbing.

I feel it in my veins.

Liquid fire.

Passion.

Driving me insane.

And the bar set so high.

Ayden has soared over.

Past the heavens.

And captured me eternally.

"Go to sleep, Lyric," he whispers, his breathing ragged.

I nod, still terrified to open my eyes. Terrified I'll lose this moment.

A moment I know I'll be able to fill pages and pages with the most powerful lyrics I've ever written. All about him and that kiss.

Chapter 11

Ayden

Therapy did not go well today, but maybe that's because I was a basket case while I was there.

"Ayden, are you sure there's nothing else you want to talk about?" my therapist had asked, chomping on a mint—the dude always has one in his mouth.

I had raked my fingers through my hair for the millionth time in the last hour. "Yeah, I'm good."

"Are you sure?" he pressed, while jotting notes down. "Are your nightmares troubling you again?"

I gripped at the wooden armrest of the chair I was sitting in. "No, they've been ... fine." A lie, but I didn't want to talk about them, because then we would have had to talk about other stuff—Lyric stuff.

He had set the pen he was writing with down. "What about flashbacks? Are you having any of those?"

I shook my head. "No, not for a while."

He overlapped his fingers on top of his organized desk, considering something. "You know I can't help you if you don't talk to me."

I wiped my sweaty palms on the front of my jeans. "I'm just stressed out over school," I had lied, to avoid what was really bothering me. Lyric. That kiss. The way our lips touched. The way my heart races in panic every time I even think about it. I could only imagine what would happen if I spoke about it aloud.

He sighed, something he did when he was letting my silence slide, yet wasn't thrilled about it.

An hour later, I'm running around my room like a chicken with its head cut off, searching for my guitar. I can't remember where I left it last night, can't remember much of anything over the last week. My thoughts are scattered, my dreams more vivid, my control gone.

All this from a kiss I can't get out of my head.

But it wasn't just the kiss. It was ...

Lips. Aching. A touch.

The contact. The connection.

The rush.

It brought my soul back

to life.

And I'm fucking terrified.

171

I haven't kissed anyone since before I was put into the system. Haven't kissed anyone because I wanted to. I've been kissed a few times—I remember that much about my past—but I can't remember exactly how they happened. Won't remember.

I had cracked open Pandora's Box with the dancing at the club, but it flew right open with the kiss. A kiss I clearly wasn't ready for, even if it was the best kiss I've ever fucking had. Life would have been a lot simpler if all my kisses were like that.

But they weren't.

And life isn't simple.

Now, I'm trapped in a scarred body that cringes whenever it has to endure human contact, except for when it comes to Lyric. I didn't cringe during that kiss. Not once. Which was good. The whole point of it was to try and erase the pain William caused from her eyes. If I could just get over the helpless, out of control fear I feel whenever I'm around her now, things will be golden.

But my soul is out.

Surfaced above the years of pain.

Fuck. I need to stop thinking.

Focus on finding my guitar. Yes, find the guitar. Much

more simple.

I look out my window toward Lyric's house. Maybe that's where I left it. But am I that desperate to go over there and find out?

Lyric suddenly appears through her window, jumping around and singing at the top of her lungs. I still have yet to hear her sing, but I can imagine the warm sound of her voice and those incredibly soft lips of hers creating striking songs.

Amazing songs.

That I want to drink out of her.

Taste.

Fuck, I'm losing my Goddamn mind.

My phone rings from my back pocket, and I let out a breath in relief at the distraction. I fish it out, figuring it's Sage calling to see if I'm on my way to band practice.

"I'm on my way now," I answer without checking my screen as I reach for my wallet on the nightstand.

"That's super awesome." It's Lyric's voice that fills the line and my heart flutters. Actually fucking flutters, like I'm some lovesick puppy. "But I just called to ask why on earth you've been staring at my bedroom window. You've been doing it for like five minutes, and it's starting to get a little bit creepy."

I frown when I spot her waving at me through her window.

"What's wrong?" she asks. "You've been acting a little strange lately. More and more like the shy boy I first met, the one who would barely utter a few stray sentences to me. I'm not losing you, am I? Because we made a deal to be friends, and my deals are unbreakable. If you want out of them, there's this big huge test I have to give you, and I know how much you hate tests."

Lyric has never mentioned a single word about the kiss, which I'm both relieved and upset about. She's been her light, full of sunshine self, acting as if she's completely unaffected.

"I'm fine. Our friendship is fine. Everything is fantastic. I promise." I turn my back to the window, silently begging for my guitar to miraculously appear in my room, but it doesn't. "I just can't find my guitar anywhere."

"That's because it's over here, you goofball. Remember, last night at family dinner when you were playing with my dad and me, which FYI totally made his day. Although he's never actually said it, I think he secretly wishes he had

174

a son sometimes. Or at least a daughter who doesn't suffer from stage fright."

"I'm sure he loves you, Lyric, whether you get over that or not."

"Of course he does. That's not what I meant. I think he's just super stoked that you could become his protégé." She lets out a wicked laugh at the end, the effortless sound splintering the weight on my chest.

"Hey, could you bring my guitar down to the driveway? I'm late for practice, and I know Sage is going to be sending me nasty texts soon."

"Sure thing, shy boy. I'll be right out."

She hangs up before I can say anything else.

I feel like banging my head on the wall, because now I've got to go down and see her again for the fiftieth time since the kiss, and I know I'm going to get all awkward again.

Get it together.

Get it together.

I grab the car keys and jog down the stairs and out to the driveway. Lyric is already waiting for me on the fence with her long legs dangling over the side and my guitar case on her lap. Her blonde hair is braided to the side, and she doesn't have a drop of makeup on, revealing her freckles and perfection.

God, she's beautiful.

"So, I was thinking," she says as I approach her, "that I could go to your practice with you."

I pause at the fence line, stuffing my wallet into my back pocket. "Why?"

She frowns as she hops off the fence. "Well, I didn't expect that sullen reaction." She shoves my guitar at me then adjusts the bottom of her purple shirt lower so her stomach is covered up. She's done that a lot over the last week. She's also worn a lot of jeans, as if trying to cover herself up more, like she blames how she dressed on what happened.

"Sorry." I grasp the handle of my guitar case. "I didn't mean it like that. It's just ... you've never wanted to go with me before, so I'm just a little confused."

She shrugs as she scuffs her boot across the ground. "I need to get out of the house. I feel like I'm losing my mind. Everywhere I go, one of my parents follows me, like they expect me to break apart at any moment. And I know they're not going to let me go anywhere unless I'm with you."

Despite the sheer awkwardness I'm feeling, I say, "You can always come with me. You know that."

She straightens her shoulders and beams at me. "Thank you. Let me go tell them where I'm going. I'll be right back." She hoists herself over the fence and sprints into her house through the side door near the garage.

With my guitar in my hand, I climb into Lila's Mercedes that she's pretty much given to me at this point. The Gregorys own two other cars, so she always acts like it's never a big deal to let me drive their extra vehicle somewhere. But it is. A. Big. Freaking. Huge. Deal. Because it means they trust me.

"Okay, I'm totally good to go," Lyric says as she slides into the passenger seat. "I just have to be back before eleven, which is so weird. I've never had a curfew before."

"I'm sure they're just worried," I tell her as I back down the driveway, pretending that I'm not hyperaware of her scent filling up the cab. God, she smells so good.

"I know that." She draws the seatbelt over her shoulder. "But I'm feeling a bit smothered ever since my parents decided to press charges against William. I'm hoping things will cool off here in a few weeks when he gets sentenced, or whatever is going to happen to him." The seatbelt clicks into place and she relaxes back in the seat. "Although, if he does get any sort of punishment, I'm sure it'll just be community service, since he doesn't have a prior."

I flip on the blinker to pull out onto the main road of our subdivision. "You say that way too casually."

"I have to be casual about it." She props her feet on the dash and reaches for the iPod docked in the middle console. "Otherwise, it'll pull me down. And I refuse to go down." She pauses as she browses through the songs. "I think my parents might be worried I have a mental illness."

"What?" I gape at her, half expecting her to insert a punch line to her joke. Because she has to be joking.

She shrugs with her head angled forward, her attention fixed on the playlists. "I heard them whispering about it the other day after I momentarily lost my shit and yelled at them."

I tap the brakes at a red light. "What did they say exactly?"

"Well, it wasn't so much *they* as it was my mother." She lifts her shoulders and shrugs. "She just seemed really

178

concerned when I burst into freaking tears for no reason."

"Was this before or after you told them about William?"

"Before. I only actually told them what happened because they seemed super twitchy about my mood swings."

I press on the gas as the light turns green. "What happened when you told them? Did they seem better about it?"

She chews on her bottom lip. "I'm not sure ... I've heard them whispering a couple of times before about my super cheery attitude. Again, it was more my mother. They never do it in front of me, but I've accidentally heard enough to know she worries about me."

"Why, though? I mean, I've lived with someone who was mentally ill, and that's not ..." I trail off.

Her concentration floats from the playlists, her eyes falling to the scars on my hand. "Was it the people who did that to you? That weird cult thing I found out about?"

I withdraw my hand and tuck it to my side. "It was."

"I'm sorry, Ayden. About everything. About showing you that tattoo thing. That I haven't found your brother for you yet."

"That's not your responsibility." I return my hand to

the wheel. "Besides, it doesn't matter. Lila told me the other day that she looked into my brother, and ... apparently he dropped out of the system a year ago. I'll more than likely never see him again."

Her eyes widen. "Oh my God, I'm so sorry."

"It's not your fault. It's ... well, it's my mother's since this whole thing started with her." My hands begin to shake on the wheel as I remember the day she handed us over to those people.

They were actually our next door neighbors, had been for a while. She needed a babysitter so she could go get her next fix. She questioned nothing, not even the chains in the living room. And they were more than willing to take us, needing their next victims.

"What about your mom?" Lyric dares ask. "What happened to her? Maybe finding her could help us find your brother and sister."

"She's dead. And I don't know who my dad is, so that won't help us either. Face it, I'll probably never get to see anyone from my family again."

"Ayden ..." She clears her throat. "You have a family. All the Gregorys love you. And ... so do I."

Breathe, breathe, breathe.

With the sound of your heart.

With the whisper of your soul.

Until everything connects.

Composes.

And creates a song.

I can't speak. Can barely breathe. Lyric's eyes refuse to leave mine, even though I'm looking everywhere but at her. I wonder if this is the time she's not going to give up, if she's going to push me until I shatter into a million pieces.

"I think my grandmother had a bipolar disorder," she says, facing forward in the seat and scrolling through the song lists again, going back to the original conversation without missing a beat. "Maybe that's why my mom worries. Perhaps she thinks I'm going to turn out like her."

Air rushes back to my lungs at the abrupt subject change.

As we reach the last house on the street, I turn into the driveway. "Why would she think that? You're like the happiest person I know." I stop at the end of the drive, shove the shifter into park, and slide the keys out of the ignition.

"Maybe I'm a little too happy, though." She places the

181

iPod on the dock without selecting a song. "Besides, some mental illnesses are hereditary."

"I know that."

"I don't believe it's fully true, though," Lyric states, drawing her sunglasses over her eyes. "I think if you don't want to turn out like your parents, then you won't. Look at my mom. She's a pretty stable woman, and I know from bits and pieces of stories I've heard that she had a pretty shitty life growing up."

I swallow the lump in my throat to stop myself from asking.

What happened to her?

Was she broken?

Is she fixed?

Saved from the darkness.

That once grasped her wrists.

"What do you think about when you daze off like that?" she asks curiously. "I've always wondered what goes on inside your head."

If she did know, she'd run.

"Nothing important." Before she can say anything else, I snatch up my guitar from the backseat and bolt out of the car.

I don't look back as I rush up the wide driveway, toward the side door of the detached garage. I free a trapped breath when I hear the car door shut. As much as my emotions are terrifying me, and as much as I know I don't deserve her to, I *need* her to follow me like my heart needs blood pumping through it.

"Hey, man," Sage greets as I stride into the shallow space of the garage. He's perched on a short stool in front of his drums, twirling the drumsticks in his hands. There's a joint burning from an ashtray on a table near a leather couch, and the air is laced with the pungent stench of weed. He does this a lot in an attempt to hotbox the garage. Says it makes him play better. The problem is, it also makes Nolan and I a little buzzed, and we definitely don't play better when we are.

"Hey." I drop the guitar down on the sofa. "Just so you know, Lyric came with me today."

He purposely drops the drumsticks and stands up. "Dude, so not cool." He heads for the joint burning in the ashtray.

"She's cool," I tell him as he puts the joint out and flips on the ceiling fan. "She won't give a shit if you're hotboxing the garage. *I* might, but she'll be fine with it."

A panicked look crosses his face as he douses the air with Lysol. "That's not what I'm worried about."

I'm so lost. Sage never gives a shit about anything, even his mom finding out he's high. "Then what are you worried about?"

He sets the can down on the table. "Don't you think Lyric's just kind of, I don't know, s—" He gets cut off as the door swings open and Lyric strolls into the room.

I start forming every *S* word I can think of.

Sunny?

Strange?

Sweet?

Sassy?

Sexy?

It better not fucking be the last one.

Lyric's nose instantly scrunches as she gets a whiff of the air. "Dude, it reeks of pot in here." She closes the door behind her and spins around to face us, her eyes skimming the room. "Is that what you guys secretly do here?" she asks suspiciously, her gaze dancing back and forth between Sage and me. "Is this whole band thing a ruse to be closet potheads?"

"Nah, Ayden doesn't do that shit," Sage tells her, leaning over to gather his drumsticks from off the floor.

"You do, though. I know that," Lyric remarks as she circles the room, studying all the framed albums on the wall. "Was your dad a musician or something?"

Sage glances at me for some reason then strolls up to her with his hands tucked into his back pockets. "Nah. He just wishes he was. And actually, the albums are my mother's. She just bought all of them a year ago after my dad cheated on her. They're all of his favorite albums signed by his favorite bands, and he will never get to see a single one of these, other than the one time my mother brought him over here to rub it in his face."

"That's so sick and twisted," Lyric mumbles as she leans forward to inspect one album in particular. "Aw, Micha Scott. He's pretty good for being old school." She casts a sly glance over her shoulder at me.

"Yeah, he's okay." Sage playfully bumps his shoulder into hers, filling me with the strangest sensation of jealousy, enough that I want to bump into him a hell of a lot harder, maybe even knock him down. "Hey, any relation?" he jokes.

"He's actually my dad."

Sage starts to laugh, but then his eyes widen when he notes the serious expression on Lyric's face. "You have got to be shitting me."

She shrugs as she scratches at her arm then rubs her eyes, probably because of the abundance of smoke swirling around the air. "Nope. I'm totally being one hundred percent shitting free serious right now."

I can't help but chuckle.

His eyes enlarge even more. "Let me get this straight. Your father is Micha Scott, rock star slash music producer who owns Infinity Studio, and he's been your father this entire time."

Lyric shrugs again, shuffling her feet back and forth across the carpet. "Yep, pretty much."

Sage shoots a baffled look at me. "Did you know about this?"

Nodding, I sink down on the couch and unlock my guitar case. "I don't know why you're freaking out so much, though."

"Um, because you have a connection," he says, confounded.

"No, Lyric has a connection." I sweep my hair out of

my face as I position my guitar on my lap. "Not me."

He shakes his head, still flabbergasted. "You could have said something at least."

"It wasn't my something to tell." I pluck my fingers across the strings, tuning the guitar while tuning Sage out.

He twists around, facing Lyric again. "So can you do anything?"

"Oh, I can do a lot of things," Lyric replies in her flirty tone that causes my jaw to tick. She plops down on the sofa beside me, slips her hands under her legs, and leans toward me, her hair brushing my cheek. Her eyes are slightly bloodshot and her pupils are unfocused.

I reach back to open the window while Sage drags a stool over to us.

"I mean, can you play anything?" Sage wonders, plopping down on the stool.

"I can play a lot of things," Lyric replies, resting her head on my shoulder.

Sage flashes me a puzzled glance and I shrug.

I have no clue what she's doing, other than maybe she's high. What I do know is that the feel of her is driving me absolutely crazy in the best way possible. Her touching me is nothing new. She's usually got her fingers laced through mine, but this feels different somehow, as if she's trying to read me through the connection of our bodies. Maybe it's all the freaking pot in the air, or maybe it's because of the kiss. I'd be fine with it—I'm usually good at keeping myself in control—but my breathing has gone erratic and my heart's lost its Goddamn mind.

"Like what?" Sage asks Lyric, reaching for the lighter on the floor near his feet.

"The violin, guitar, drums. I used to play the piano, but I haven't practiced in a while."

"What about singing?"

She hesitates. "Singing is subjective, so I can't answer that."

Sage assesses her closely. "So, you're saying you think you can sing, but you're unsure of your voice." He flicks his lighter on and off as he deliberates something. Then he hops to his feet and ambles over to the microphone. Picking it up off the floor, he twists up the volume of the speaker. "Let's see what you got, Scott." He tosses the microphone at Lyric.

As she catches it, her face drains of color. "Um, I'm not going to sing for you." She chucks the microphone at him. Instead of catching it, Sage skitters out of the way and it ends up crashing against the symbols.

All three of us stare at it as it threatens to topple over.

He rips his focus off the vibrating metal. "Why not?"

Lyric glances at me for help, but I have no idea what to say to her. I've never heard her sing. Hell, she barely lets me hear her play the guitar and she rocks at that. But I know she does it all, sings, plays, writes lyrics.

"I'd really like to hear the answer myself," I tell her, shifting the guitar off my lap. "Because I've been really curious for a while."

She glares at me, and I shrink back. "I already told you I have stage fright."

Right. She has told me that. Maybe I'm higher than I thought.

Sage flicks his hand at her, waving her off. "That is totally curable."

Lyric crosses her legs, and her gaze glides across Sage's facial piercings. "And what's your cure? Should I dye my hair and pierce my skin to make me believe I'm a true rock star?"

Sage points at his chest. "I'm not a rock star. I can't

sing at all, but I can play the drums like a badass."

Lyric folds her arms across her chest with a sway of attitude in her body. "So can I."

I catch Sage peeking at her cleavage popping out of her shirt. That's when I realize the *S* word he was about to drop when Lyric walked in was probably sexy. It pisses me off, and my reaction is surprising as shit.

But Lyric isn't sexy. She's fun, ridiculously happy, effortlessly beautiful, life-saving, and mind-blowingly amazing. Sexy doesn't even begin to sum her up.

"Yeah, but our band doesn't need a drummer." He scoops up the microphone from the floor and presents it to her like it's a bouquet. "We need a singer."

Lyric folds her fingers around the mic as she takes it from him. "I can't. I'll seriously throw up if I even try."

He holds up a finger as a slow grin curves at his lips. "I have an idea for that."

When he disappears through a door at the back of the room, I say to Lyric, "You don't have to do it. Sage just gets crazy about this stuff. He lives and breathes music and thinks everyone should do the same."

"I live and breathe music, too," Lyric reminds me, anxiously chewing on her bottom lip. "I just can't do it in public... You really think he's got some magical cure for stage fright?"

I line my fingers against the guitar strings and strum a chord. "Probably not. But if he does come out with a brownie, please don't eat it."

"I won't, but I think I might be a little bit high already."

"Yeah, me, too."

A nervous giggle escapes her lips then she relaxes back on the sofa and kicks up her feet on the stool. "So, can I ask you something?"

My fingers tense and I miss the next chord. "I guess so."

"It's about the other night ... about the ... kiss." She pauses, and an enormous lump wedges in my throat. "I think it might be the weed talking, because I promised myself I wasn't going to bring it up, but now I suddenly feel like I need to."

I squeeze my eyes shut. I still have my head down so she can't see my face. Thank God, or otherwise, who the hell knows what she would see.

"I just wanted to make you feel better about that asshole stealing your first kiss," I say, messing around with the knob on the bottom of the guitar. "It was the only thing I could think of to do."

Liar.

In the darkness.

You are.

The biggest.

Liar I've ever seen.

Pretend it doesn't exist.

Like everything else inside you.

She cracks her knuckles. "So it was just a friend kiss, then? Because Maggie has a theory that our friendship might have blossomed into love." She laughs like she thinks the idea is funny.

Me, I find it terrifying.

Love.

The word souls burn for.

People die for.

Live for.

Breathe for.

But for me, it's simply poetry, lyrics, an emotion I'll never understand.

Can't.

I swallow hard and force my voice to be equally as light. "Yeah, of course. And I really think you should stop listening to Maggie. It's what started the whole thing with William to begin with."

"Hey." She cups my chin and forces me to look up at her. "I'm totally cool with you kissing me to cheer me up, just as long as we stay friends. I never want anything to get weird between us."

"Of course." I bob my head up and down. "I want the same thing."

"Good." She smiles as she reclines back in the seat.

The scatteredness in my head begins to clear. This was my problem—it had to be. I was so worried I'd lose her as a friend that it fucked with my head. Thank God, I'm cured.

"You and I"—she points back and forth between us— "we're going to be one of those people who are still friends when we're super old, like our parents." A laugh bubbles from my lips and her smile expands. "You know, I always feel so special whenever I get you to smile. Like I discovered some sort of rare gem."

I want to kiss her right there, eternally seal my lips to hers.

Okay, maybe I'm not cured.

Maybe I can't be cured.

Of anything.

"You're special, Lyric. You should know that by now."

"So are you." She pats my leg then rises to her feet when Sage strolls back into the room.

"So, what's your huge plan to cure me?" she asks him.

He holds up a brownie in his hand. "This will cure all your stage fright." He draws and X over his heart and winks at her. "I promise."

Shaking my head, I set my guitar down and rise to my feet. "No way." I push Sage's hand back. "How about I blow off practice and we do something fun," I suggest to Lyric. "Nolan isn't even here anyway."

"He's always late," Sage intervenes, munching on the brownie. "He'll show up in like ten minutes or so."

"I was kind of hoping coming here would cure me of my stage fright." Lyric stares at me with hope in her eyes. "I don't know why, but I thought it would help somehow, like maybe being around you and seeing how much fun you guys have when you play would force me to conquer my fear."

I rub my jawline, trying to conjure up an idea. I remember when I was afraid of the dark, how I used to cover my ears and shut my eyes to block out my surroundings. It didn't cure me, but it got me through the night. Now I use music and that silly nightlight Lyric gave me forever ago.

"I have an idea," I say, my voice unsteady from a memory long forgotten of me as a small boy begging to be let free. "But it might be a little weird."

She smiles excitedly. "Lay it on me. Whatever it is, I trust you, Ayden."

Her words crash into my heart, more than in a just-friends way. I wonder just how much of a lie I told her when I said that it was just a friend kiss. It doesn't matter, though. Lyric is the sunshine in my world. She keeps me going when things get really dark. I'm not even ready for a relationship. I can barely handle myself right now, even something as simple as kissing her sent me into panic attack after panic attack.

I suddenly realize something makes my scars throb, that I'm not ready to handle the emotions clipping their way to the surface. That even though I have a new life, the cuffs and chains are still there, trying to pull me down into the darkness of memories, begging to haunt me. Of myself. My brother. My sister.

What was done to me? Stuff I can't even remember, but can somehow still feel the fear connected to the experiences.

And I'm not sure if I'll ever fully be able to escape them.

Chapter 12

Lyric

In the silence of my soul, there is a breathless ache

desperately seeking air.

Like I'm dead, yet alive.

Breathing yet suffocating.

Then I felt your lips.

The softest touch

kissed my mouth,

and my soul sang to life.

For the very first time

you showed me a taste of life.

That's what I wrote after Ayden kissed me. That's what constantly floods my thoughts day and night, over and over again. I want another taste of it—of what his kiss brought me. But he's been acting so strange since it happened. Twitchy. Smiling less. And I have no idea how to act around him other than be super happy twenty-four seven, even after what I discovered about him tonight while searching around on the internet—an article about his past.

"Are you sure about this?" I ask Ayden as I stand in the middle of the room with my eyes closed. I have earplugs in my ears, a microphone in my hand, and my heart's thudding like a jackhammer.

"Not really!" he shouts out. "But it doesn't hurt to try it out!"

"True." I dither, trying to decide if I want to do this.

Suddenly his fingers circle my wrists, and I feel his face dip toward my ear. "Relax. It's just me and Sage in the room. Two people. That's all." His breath is hot on my cheek, making the air sweltering.

I nod as my fingers grasp the microphone. "Okay."

"Okay, you're ready to do this?"

I nod then fist bump the air. I hear him chuckle, but the sound gets lost as he moves away from me.

A heartbeat or two later, the music is cranked up. Lyrics by Flyleaf surround me and it's perfect. I know for a fact that Ayden picked out this song, because he knows how much I love the band. The thought relaxes me for about two seconds until it's time for me to sing then my voice locks up in my throat.

Shit. I'm so going to throw up.

My eyelids start to lift up as panic sets in, but warm

fingers touch my wrists again.

"Relax!" Ayden shouts over the music. "I've got your back, dude."

I snort a laugh then relax.

Calm. That's all I feel.

I don't know why, but I open my eyes.

My gaze meets Ayden's grey eyes.

I think about the lyrics I wrote the other day.

My inspiration.

The stuff I dreamed about for years.

Friends or not, I'm using our kiss to my benefit.

I put the microphone up to my mouth.

Then I start to sing.

I sing like my life depends on it. Sing like I've always dreamed of doing. Sing as though my heart is going to burst if I don't scream out every emotion through the lyrics.

I'll admit, for the first thirty seconds or so, my voice is wobbly and off pitch. I start to grow concerned that maybe my life dream of singing is going to be a behind-closed-doors sort of thing. I pop the earplugs out, so I can hear myself. It helps. My voice gains stability. I unstiffen. Loosen up.

I begin dancing around the room, and Ayden laughs at me, his smile so bright his eyes crinkle around the corners. There's something in his expression, something I've never seen before, and it causes the room to spin. So I spin with it, jumping up and down, belting out the lyrics until I finally let go and get really crazy.

I shove Ayden back on the sofa and straddle his lap, singing and putting on a show for him. His eyes widen at my overly friendly touch, and his arms tense out to the side. I'm excited, rubbing my hands up and down his chest, thinking about that kiss, how amazing it was, how it exceeded the bar I set and then some. If only I could have him, but after what I found out ... I'm not sure I ever can.

I know I'm pushing him right now, and usually I'd stop, but I can't stop. I love this moment. Touching him. Singing. Being in the moment. So I keep going, shoving aside any self-protest until the song ends.

And the moment ends.

And I feel so sad for him again.

I'm sweating, exhausted, and fucking content as I climb off Ayden's lap.

"So, how'd I do?" I pant, moving the microphone away from my mouth.

Sage is staring at me with his arms crossed over his chest. I don't know him well enough to read him, but if I had to guess, he kind of looks impressed.

Sage trades a questioning look with Ayden. "You think we could rock the girl singer image?"

I sternly point at Sage. "Don't insult my girliness. I rocked the crap out of that song."

He fiddles with one of his eyebrow rings. "That you did." His eyes scroll over me then he sticks out his hand. "What do you say, Lyric? You want to be the singer of Hearts and Scars."

I'm starting to reach out to take his hand, but withdraw. "I will, but on one condition."

His expression twists with confusion. "And what's that?"

"We totally change the name to something way less cliché."

"Change the name? Are you kidding me? We spent two months coming up with that name."

"And it sucks balls, so maybe you should let me come up with one. I can even ask my dad for input," I add enticingly.

His eyes light up as he considers my offer. "All right, you have a deal, Lyric."

We shake on it, and he holds onto my hand way longer than necessary. Who knows why, nor do I care.

I turn to Ayden, grinning like an idiot. He doesn't seem as happy about the agreement as I am, though.

"What's wrong, shy boy?" I wipe the sweat from my brow.

He collects his guitar from the couch. "Nothing."

My hand falls to my side. "I totally should have asked you if you were okay with this, right?"

"Why wouldn't I be okay with this?" He slides the guitar strap over his head with his head down, his black hair shielding his eyes from my view.

"Because this is your guy thing." I gesture around the garage. "And I just crashed it with my girliness." Or is it about my inappropriate touching?

He shakes his head. "I can assure you that's the last thing I was thinking. I love your girliness."

"Then what are you thinking?" I smooth my thumb between his brows, trying to erase his worry.

His fingers strangle the guitar. "Lyric, I think we should—"

Sage clears his throat from behind us. "Nolan just pulled up." He points over his shoulder, appearing uncomfortable as fuck, like he just caught Ayden and I having sex. "You two better be ready to play."

"Okay." I direct my attention back to Ayden. "What were you going to say?"

"Nothing." Ayden strains a smile. "I'm fine. I promise. Now quit worrying and go rock your ass off." He plugs the cord into the amp and focuses on tuning his guitar.

I hate this. This last week has sucked big time, and now he suddenly seems even quieter. I want my Ayden back.

"Are you sure you're sure?"

All he does is nod.

It hurts that he might be upset with me. Makes me want to curl up in a ball and cry.

But Nolan strolls in before I can utter a word.

"Who's fucking ready to get this...?" He trails off mid-sentence as he kicks the door shut. "Why are you here?"

From what I understand, Nolan rocks the bass. He looks more like a lead singer in a boy band than anything. Spikey blond hair, blue eyes, these crazy full lips that don't seem like they should belong to a guy, yet they do. He wears a lot of skinny jeans, too, and fitted shirts, more hipster than rock star.

"Wow, hello to you, too," I joke as I rotate the volume knob on the amp.

He rolls his eyes as he shucks off his jacket then drapes it on a hook near the door. "As much as I adore you, Lyric, I don't find your sarcasm funny."

I pull a face. I've known Nolan since ninth grade, and while we're not technically friends, I know him well enough that I can mess around with him. "Yes, you do. Don't lie."

He snorts a laugh as he weaves around the sofa to collect his guitar from the corner of the room. "Fine, you're amusing." He picks up the guitar and slides the handle over his head. "But seriously, why are you here?"

"Because she's our new singer," Sage intervenes as he materializes from the back room with another brownie in his hand.

"Really?" Nolan asks, glancing from Sage to Ayden, then his gaze lands on me. "You decided to follow in your father's footsteps, then, huh? I'm crossing my fingers you can sing as good as him."

"Of course I can," I say confidently, but my stage fright momentarily creeps in and puts the tiniest hint of doubt in me.

"You knew who her father was, too?" Sage asks incredulously as he heads for the amp.

Nolan shrugs. "I thought everyone did."

"I guess I'm the only idiot out of the loop, then," Sage mutters as he nibbles on the brownie.

"Are you cool with me being part of the band?" I ask Nolan, because I know enough about bands to understand my initiation will only work if they're all on the same page.

He briefly contemplates my question, but the hesitancy is more for show than anything. Because moments later, he grins and pats me on the arm. "Of course. Welcome to the band. Now, let's get this show on the road and see what you got." He plugs his amp in and twists up the volume.

I try to catch Ayden's eye as I move the microphone up to my mouth to sing, but he keeps his chin down, his eyes focused on the guitar strings.

I spend the next hour singing my heart out with the guys, doing my best not to focus on Ayden and instead on the music. By the time we're finished with practice, my lungs ache in the best way possible.

The drive home is soundlessly painful, though. Ayden will barely utter a word to me. I grow more anxious that the kiss might have changed our friendship in a negative way, but at the same time, I'm excited that I was able to sing and finally found a band to be part of.

By the time we pull up in the driveway, I'm ready to bounce into the house and announce the news to my dad.

"That was so much fun," I tell Ayden as he shuts the headlights off. "Thank you for letting me tag along. You should come up to my room and watch a movie with me. We can celebrate." I cross my fingers, praying he will.

He shakes his head, rotating around and reaching into the backseat for his guitar. "I can't. I have homework." He hurries out of the car and up the driveway toward the house.

"Was it because I sucked?" I call out in desperation as I stumble out of the car and out beneath the stars. "Was Sage just being nice and I'm really not that good?"

He pauses then gradually turns around. When the porch light hits his face, I can see the shock in his eyes.

"Lyric, you have a fucking beautiful voice. It's crazy how amazing it is ... unreal. But I ..." He appears completely terrified as he turns away and rushes into the house, shutting the door behind him and leaving his words echoing in my head.

A beautiful voice.

That someone can finally hear.

Let my words spill out into the world.

Let my soul drench the air.

Let it change lives.

Let it bring my best friend back.

But he doesn't come back, and I stand alone in the dark, desperate to chase after him, yet terrified what will happen if I do.

I turn for the door and trudge into my house, less eager to tell my dad the news now. I honestly think about going straight up to my room, but my parents are at the kitchen table eating cake when I walk in.

"Hey, sweetie," my mom says, but instantly frowns when she sees the look on my face. It's the same expression she wore when I had my meltdown the other day. They had both looked at me like I was going to liquefy into a crazy puddle on the hardwood floor. One day I will make her confess why she looks at me that way sometimes. "What happened?"

Sinking into the chair, I reach across the table to steal a glob of pink frosting from her slice of cake. "Nothing. Ayden and I are just having a little spat." If I can even call it that. I honestly have no clue what the hell is going on in that boy's head anymore.

"I'm sorry." My mother discreetly glances at my father as he shovels a chunk of cake into his mouth. "But don't worry, you two will get over it. Best friends always do."

"Ayden and I aren't you and Dad, Mom." I lick the frosting from my finger. "We just ..." I trail off. We just what? Spend every waking hour together? Kiss in the darkness of the room? Sing solo performances while grinding on each other. "So, I have some news." I change the subject. "I'm officially a singer in a band."

My dad's back straightens, and he beams with pride. "Oh, really? When did this happen?"

I shrug as I roam over to the cupboard. "Tonight. One of Ayden's band members convinced me to sing, although Ayden was the one who actually helped me." I grab a glass from the cupboard then open the fridge. "But it doesn't matter. The important thing is I'm officially cured of my stage fright and can live out my lifelong dream." When I remove the jug of milk out of the fridge, I notice how edgy my father is. "What's wrong, weirdo Dad?"

"It's nothing." He takes a swig of his milk. "It's just that ... I just want to make sure you're careful. If you really get into this band thing ... well, the environment is intense."

My mom nods in agreement. "It's not that we don't trust you, but we just want to make sure you don't get into too much trouble."

"I get into trouble all the time," I remind them as I fill the glass with milk. "But if you're talking about drugs, sex, rock 'n' roll, and all that shit, you should know I'm good with staying away from that stuff."

"Okay, but there will be rules," she says as she cuts into the slice of cake in front of her.

"What exactly do you guys think I'm doing?" I ask as I take a seat again. "I just joined the band; I'm not starring on stage yet."

"But if it's your lifelong dream, you will eventually," my father chimes in. "And I just want to make sure you do things the right way."

"Like using my father's awesome connections to get

my foot in the door?" I grin sweetly at him.

He tries not to smile, but it slips through. "Maybe. I'll have to hear you play first."

I press my hand to my chest, mocking being offended. "Father, I'm shocked. You seriously don't believe that with my awesome genetics, I don't have the voice of an angel." He wavers, and I throw a napkin at his face. "So insulting." I rise from my chair. "I'm going to bed. I'll let you two finish off your cake."

When I get to my room, though, I don't go to sleep. I write.

Kiss me goodnight. Throw me away.

Hug me tight. Then let me fray.

Pieces of you. Unraveling me.

Weakening, so desperate to be free.

Ready to break. Ready to tear.

I can see you breaking, and it's so hard to bear.

I finish the last sentence then peek out my window at Ayden's home. The lights in his room are off, but I'm only half convinced he's asleep, since his room isn't glowing with the black light I gave him.

I move over to my desk and open up the webpage I was looking at earlier today before I went to band practice.

I'd been so shocked when I found it that I actually had to get up and scream the lyrics of the most intense, angry song I could find, just to feel like I could breathe again.

After months of investigating, I finally managed to find an article that I think was linked to Ayden's past. It happened in San Diego, and there's a mention of a woman that has the same last name as Ayden's old one who died.

After a complaint was made about noise disruption, police were led to a home where three abused children were found, appearing to be beaten and starved. No arrests have been made, but the case is heavily under investigation. While reports haven't been confirmed, the case has been linked to three other abuse cases in the area over the last three years. All the victims suffered from the same injuries and subjection.

It makes me wonder exactly what happened to Ayden. Makes me afraid for him. Makes me wonder if the people who tortured him were ever captured.

Is that why he's always afraid?

Or is it something else?

Something worse.

Chapter 13

Ayden

Even though it's killing me, I've been keeping my distance from Lyric. It's almost impossible, though, when she lives right next door and our families spend a hell of a lot of time together. Plus, there's the whole band thing. Whenever we practice, she's there, and Sage is there staring at her. The dude clearly has a thing for her. Thankfully, she doesn't seem too interested.

I'm not going to lie, I'm fucking miserable. I miss her way more than I thought was ever possible. But I can't help my distant behavior.

That night Lyric sang, jumping on my lap and touching me, caused me to shrink within myself, because I liked it. Wanted more. And it fucking terrified me as I remembered what more felt like.

I remember the touches that singed my skin.

The way they touched me.

How I begged them to stop.

But my voice was hollow.

Resonating.

A sound no one seemed to hear.

The world was merely a shadow

as they tied me up.

Cuffed me.

Used me.

Drained my soul.

Spilled my blood into the earth.

Then left me for dead.

To rot away with the others.

Rot away with their sins.

"Ayden, did you hear me?"

I focus back on reality as I listen to my band members, trying to figure out a plan that will get our foot in the door of the music industry.

"We should definitely have a talk with Lyric's dad," Sage puts in his two cents as he puts away his guitar.

"Wow," Lyric states, appearing offended. "Sometimes I feel like I'm being used for my dad's connections."

Sage swiftly shakes his head. "No. Not at all." He props his guitar against the wall then faces her. "You have a killer voice, Lyric. Seriously. We're going to be badass." He scratches at the corner of his bloodshot eye. "I'm just saying that we shouldn't waste a good connection like that."

Lyric unplugs the microphone and winds up the cord. "Well, I'll bring it up to him, but he won't do anything until he hears us. We have to be good."

"We are good," Sage presses, checking out her ass as she bends over to stick the microphone onto the bottom shelf of a cupboard. When he notices that I catch him, he offers me a tense smile and shrugs, like *what are you going to do?*

"Yeah, we'll see." Lyric stands upright, tugs the elastic out of her hair, and then combs her fingers through her locks as she ponders over something.

Even though I've tried not to, I end up zoning in on her every move, the relaxed expression on her face, the way her chest arches the slightest bit, the way her glossy lips part ...

"What do you think, Ayden?" Lyric asks me as she gathers her hair back into a messy bun on her head and secures it with the elastic.

I realize I'm staring at her, holding my breath, and clutching the life out of my guitar.

"About what?" I ask her dazedly.

She holds my gaze, silently begging for something I don't fully understand, nor do I think I can give to her. "About asking my dad for help?"

I shrug as I slide the guitar strap over my head. "If you want to, then do it. I'm sure he'll be okay with it." I don't look at her as I speak. Instead, I concentrate on putting my guitar away, checking my phone, the clock, anything to keep me busy, hyperaware that she's watching me, like she has every day at practice and at school. Our time has only been filled with formal conversation and polite smiles, and I think it's starting to get to her. It's definitely starting to get to me.

"I have to go," I lie when her stare becomes unbearable. "I have some stuff I'm supposed to do at home."

I continue to feel her eyes on me as I hurry across the room, grab my jacket, and dart out the door. Only when I step out into the cool night air can I breathe again.

Lyric and I haven't been driving to band practice or school together, so I make the short drive home by myself, with only my thoughts for company. I'm lonely. Sad. Lost.

On the one hand, I want to remain in my little bubble, because it's easier to breathe and exist. Then again, my bubble isn't really giving me the shelter it used to. It was easier being lonely when that was all I knew. Now that I've gotten a taste of the other side, where I can coexist with people, putting myself in solitude isn't as simple.

By the time I arrive home, I'm miserable and sullen. Lila notices my depression the moment I trudge into the house—she has for the last couple of weeks now. Like always, she convinces me to help her out with something to keep me from locking myself into my room.

"Help me bake Everson's birthday cake," she tells me when I wander into the kitchen, looking for something to eat.

"I'm not that good at baking," I point out as I hunt the cupboards for something to fill my appetite. "Remember when I tried to make those cookies?"

She kindly smiles as she pulls out a carton of eggs from the fridge. "I'll put you on egg duty. It's hard to mess that up."

Closing the cupboard, I take a seat on the barstool and do what she asks, breaking and separating eggshells. Something in the process and the way the yolk falls out of the egg strikes up a distant memory.

Thick, like yolk.

I watch the blood drip.

Over and over.

A repeated pattern.

Driving me mad.

The way it splatters.

Across the floor.

The sound is like nails.

Pounding into my skull.

Drip. Drip. Drip.

Even when I shut my eyes

the dripping still exists.

Over and over.

Never a miss.

I'd lift my hands.

Cover my ears.

Suffocating the dripping out.

But my wrists are tied.

Weighed to the ground.

So I'm stuck

with the torture

weighing me down.

"Ayden, did you hear me?" Lila asks.

I flinch out of my daze, returning back to reality. What

I'm supposed to be doing. The food on the counter. The eggs in front of me.

"Um, no, I didn't. Sorry." I pick up an egg and crack the shell against the edge of the bowl while she turns down the heat on the stove.

I'm not sure why I suddenly remembered the sound of the blood dripping, or who the blood even belonged to. I wish I could figure out why I'm having a sudden onset of memories so I could come up with a way to forget again.

"I asked you if you wanted to go help Lyric and her dad work on the car he bought her." She moves a pan of boiling water to an unheated burner. "I'm sure cooking is getting boring."

I split the egg apart and let the yolk drip into the bowl. "Nah, I'm cool here."

Trepidation creases her face. "Are you sure? Because you seem like you're not having that much fun."

"I'm fine." I set the eggshells down on the counter and wipe my fingers on a paper towel.

She dithers, pulling a drawer open to retrieve a spoon. "You and Lyric seem … I don't know. Did you have a fight or something?"

"No." It's technically not a lie. We're not exactly fighting. I'm just avoiding her. And she's tried to get me to talk to her. A lot.

"Then why aren't you two hanging out anymore?"

"I don't know."

She's growing frustrated, her cheeks reddening. "Well, I don't care what's going on." She suddenly goes from kind, caring mom to annoyed, get-your-shit together mom, a side I've never seen before. She shoves a plate full of cookies into my hand and shoos me toward the door. "You will go over, and give Lyric and her father some of these cookies."

She has got to be shitting me.

"But—"

"No buts," she cuts me off, snapping her fingers as she points toward the doorway. "Either you go over there, or I make you go talk to the therapist. Maybe he can get to the bottom of why you two suddenly aren't speaking to each other."

Unsure how to respond, I do as she says and start for the backdoor.

"Oh, someone got in trouble, didn't they?" Fiona teases as we cross paths in the foyer. She's got her dark brown hair up in butterfly clips, and her lips stained a fiery red that match her dress.

"Does Lila know you're wearing that much makeup?" I ask as I maneuver the door open, letting the cool November breeze gust in.

She blows me a kiss. "Of course." She's probably lying, though, and will also lie her way out of it when Lila gets mad at her. "Oh, and make sure to make up with Lyric while you're over at her house. I'm seriously getting tired of your sulking." She flashes me a crafty grin then skips out of the foyer and into the kitchen.

Painfully aware of how much I've changed over the last few weeks, I step outside and shut the door behind me.

The sun is set, the sky black. Almost every house on the street is lit up with Christmas lights and flashing signs that promise Christmas cheer. I'm not a big fan of the holidays, but I've gotten better over the last year that I've spent with the Gregorys. I've gotten better at a lot of things while living with them. I just wish things could have remained that way. That the memories had stayed locked away, instead of clawing their way back into my mind.

The garage door of Lyric's house is open when I round

the fence. Light and music filters into the night, engulfing me the moment I step foot on the property. The sight of Lyric slams against my chest as the kiss we shared a month ago overwhelms me.

I almost spin around and run, but Lyric spots me and waves.

"Hey," she says in astonishment when I approach the open garage. Her hair is braided, and she's wearing a leather jacket, holey pants, and black lace-up boots. Her cheeks are flushed, and her lips are tinted blue from the chilly breeze.

"Hey," is all I can think of to say back, because I can still feel it. That stupid flutter in my heart, the one that showed up after we kissed. And the emotions associated to the last time someone kissed me.

She sets down a wrench she's holding and meets me around the back of the car. Her gaze drops to the plate in my hand. "Did you bring me cookies?"

I stare at her for way longer than necessary, only ripping my gaze away when she looks up at me. "Oh, yeah, Lila sent them over."

"Can I have one?" she asks, acting coyer than normal. "A cookie, I mean."

"Yeah, of course." My fingers fumble as I lift the plastic off the plate.

She selects one of the snowmen caked in frosting and sprinkles. "These look so good." She dunks her fingertip in the frosting and licks it off, causing a rush of adrenaline to pulsate through my body.

God, I want her.

I need to get out of here.

"Is your dad around?" I frantically scan the garage. "I was supposed to give the plate to him."

She bites off the head of the snowman. "Nope, he ran out to get a part for my car," she replies with her mouth full. "Hey, do you want to see my car? I know you've been … busy, and haven't had a chance to see it yet."

"I really need to get back to the house." I set the plate of cookies on the trunk of the car, ready to bail.

"Ayden, please don't leave," she begs, nearly splitting my heart in two.

I freeze. It's the last thing my sister said to me that day we were split apart.

When I glance over my shoulder and see the tears in her eyes, I whirl around. "Lyric, I don't …" I trail off, my mind racing with what to say to her. When I come up with nothing, I cautiously inch toward her. "I'm sorry. Please don't cry. I'm so fucking sorry."

She sucks back the tears as she stares at the star dusted sky. "I just don't understand," she says, dabbing her fingertips under her eyes, wiping away some smeared eyeliner before she looks at me again. "You just stopped talking to me for almost a month, with no explanation. And I don't know how to fix it—fix us."

"It's not your fault," I promise her. "I'm just ... confused."

I let her twine our fingers together, even though her touch makes me ache all the way down to my bones.

"About what?" she asks. When I open my mouth to give her a vague answer, she cuts me off, like she knew what I was going to say before I spoke it. "You know you can tell me anything, right? I got your back, dude, remember?"

Unable to help it, I crack a smile. "Yeah, I remember. Anyone who messes with me gets a basketball to the face."

She laughs then tugs me into the garage toward a rustic 1970 something Dodge Challenger with a dented fender, bumper, hood, dented everything really. "Come on. Come see my new ride. I've been dying to show it off to you."

I allow her to lead me to the car and push me down into the passenger seat. Then she skips around the back, swiping another cookie before dropping down into the driver's seat.

"So, what do you think?" She pats the top of the torn steering wheel. "Pretty beat up, right? But it makes it so much more super awesome. My dad promised that we'd have it finished before graduation."

"Seven months, huh?" I cock a brow at the tattered backseat and caved in bodywork.

"Hey, he's really good with cars." She playfully pinches my arm then frowns when I flinch. Still, she manages to put on the nicest fake smile I've ever seen. "So is your dad."

"Who …? Oh, you mean Ethan. Yeah, I've seen some photos of the cars he used to fix up. They're pretty cool."

She rests back in her seat with her head turned toward me. "You should have him fix one up for you, then we can be twins." She wiggles her fingers in my direction. "Remember the black nail polish we were both wearing the first day you came here."

I smile at the memory. "You seemed so proud of the fact that we matched."

"I was proud," she admits, tucking a strand of hair behind her ear. She flutters her eyelashes as she peers up at me, but I can't tell if it's intentional or not. "You were so intimidating that day. I needed something to say to you."

"Intimidating?" I snort a laugh, the sound echoing around us. "You seemed so at ease. I was the one who felt intimidated."

"But you kept staring at me."

"Not at you. At your eyes. They were—are"—I shrug—"beautiful."

"You've said that to me a lot lately," she whispers softly. "At least, before you stopped talking to me."

"I'm sorry, Lyric. It's just ..." I start to get choked up. "There are still so many things you don't know about me— that I don't even know about me. If you did, you probably wouldn't want to be my friend anymore."

"Try me." When I gape at her, she sits up and props her elbows on the console. "How will you ever know the answer to that if you don't tell me stuff?"

I scratch at my arm, feeling fidgety and erratic. "I can't tell you everything. I can't even tell myself everything. But

... the whole touching thing freaks me out."

"I know it does," she says simply. "I could tell that from the first day we met."

"I don't even know why it does. I mean, sometimes I see things, and ..." I jerk my fingers through my hair. "I just feel all wrong inside."

"Ayden, I get that you've been through stuff, but I want you to always trust me. This whole fighting thing ... well, it's been killing me. The last month without you has been killing me."

"I wasn't fighting with you." My voice weakens as she leans in, as if she's about to hug me. All my instincts scream at me to back away, but I can't move. All the emotions I've been running away from emerge and magnify, more potent and toxic than ever. "I was just confused ... about stuff." As she moves in to wrap her arms around me, something crumbles inside me—my self-control.

Before I can even comprehend what I'm doing, I angle my head to the side and press my lips to hers. She tenses, but only for a fleeting second, then she melts into my touch. I realize right then and there that I can keep running from her, but I can't run away from my emotions. They'll always exist under the surface, maybe even longer than I'll admit.

"Oh my God," she groans against my lips as I slide my tongue into her mouth.

She taste like frosting and feels so warm. My fingers begin to shake as I place my hands on her waist, needing her closer, yet fearing her closeness. I grab at her shirt, both pushing and pulling her against me while I kiss her with passion, heat, trying to suffocate the memories that scar my mind.

But they mix together.

Light and dark.

Fear and lust.

Liquid and fire.

I can't get enough.

Yet I have too much.

I'm overflowing.

About to combust.

I start to protest, push back, because my mind is going into overdrive, but suddenly Lyric scrambles over the console and straddles my lap. Her warmth drowns me, seeps through my skin, and singes my veins. And when she presses her chest against mine, all the cold inside me flares.

I tangle my fingers through her hair, tugging at the roots, and slide my hand up the front of her shirt.

"Ayden." She bites at my lip, causing my entire body to quiver.

I'm so confused.

My mind wants one thing.

My body the other.

Fear.

Want.

Fear.

Want.

Past.

Future.

She rolls her hips against mine, and I gasp in desperation. In desire. In a million things I don't understand. My body feels like it's about to explode as my fingers inch up the bottom of her bra, and then graze her nipple. I have no clue what I'm doing. Absolutely no idea. *Want.* I know that I want something, so I continue to caress her, gasping and groaning as her nipple hardens under my touch. She bites at my bottom lip again, stabs her nails into my arms, holding onto me, or holding me up—I'm not sure.

I've never purposefully touched a woman like this. Feared it for three years. Yet I want to touch Lyric more than I've wanted to touch anyone, so I cup her breast, feel her delicate flesh, and lick her soft lips. She tastes so good, her skin is so warm, and the whimpers coming from her make my heart slam against my chest, almost painfully.

I'm not sure how long it goes on, us in the car, exploring each other, but it feels like forever.

I could have gone on forever.

Eventually, Lyric pulls away, but keeps her forehead pressed against mine as she traces a finger up and down the back of my neck.

"I've missed you," she utters with her eyes shut. "I'm sorry I upset you."

"I've missed you, too," I openly admit as I struggle to get oxygen into my lungs. "But it wasn't your fault I got upset. I was—am just confused."

Her eyelids lift open and she leans back. "About what?"

"About ... stuff. There's things about me, Lyric, that even I don't understand sometimes."

"You know you can tell me, right? Tell me anything."

"I wish I could ... but I can't even remember everything myself."

Strangely, she looks terrified, her eyes widening. "I've been trying to figure out how to bring this up to you, but right before you stopped talking to me, I found an article on the internet that I think is about you."

I swallow hard, scared to death, yet needing to know. "What did it say?"

She secures her arms around me, as if she's afraid I'm going to run. "It just talked about three kids being pulled out of a house. That they ... had some injuries."

"Lots of injuries," I whisper, scared to death that this conversation is going to trigger what happened before I was pulled out of that house. "More than I think the reporters realized."

Her chest rises and falls as she fights to breathe evenly, her sympathetic gaze drowning me in emotions I can barely comprehend. "Ayden, I ..." She trails off as her gaze wanders to something over my shoulder.

"What are you looking at?" I track her gaze out the rear window and see a cop car pulling up to my home.

All the fear I had been battling suddenly explodes and smothers me.

Jessica Sorensen

Chapter 14

Lyric

For once, I can't think of a single word to say. Can't smile. Can't breathe.

Everything had been so perfect for about five minutes. That kiss and those touches were the kind that artists crave, like a drug addiction. The moment was perfect, and a song was already forming in my head.

Then the cop car had pulled up to the house and everything went to shit.

I followed Ayden over to his house when he jumped out of the car. Then I sat in the living room with Lila, Ethan, and Ayden while the police started talking. My mom and dad quickly took Kale, Everson, and Fiona out of the house when they realized what the conversation was about.

They found Ayden's brother. Not just found, but discovered his body in a ditch not too far away from their childhood home. And from what it sounds like, he might have been murdered. There is an ongoing investigation, and while they didn't flat out say it, I got the impression that his

233

brother's death might have had something to do with what-ever happened to them a few years ago, that there were some marks on his body that led them to believe this, along with some other evidence they wouldn't divulge.

"If you can think of anything at all," the taller of the two officers says, directing his question to Ayden as he hands a card to Lila. "I know in the initial investigation you told the detective that you couldn't remember anything, but if you do, please call us."

"Of course," Lila replies, tucking the card in her pocket, struggling to keep it together.

"And you might want to be a bit more cautious over the next few weeks while we gather more evidence," he tells Lila as she walks them to the door. "It's just a precautionary measure, but it's better to be safe."

I try to catch Ayden's eye as Lila finishes chatting with the officers, but he won't look at me. Won't look at anything, except the scars on his hands.

Lila is sobbing by the time she returns to the living room. Ethan looks like he's about to throw up. And I feel as sick as Ethan looks.

"I'm going to go do my homework." Ayden abruptly stands up from the sofa and walks out of the room at a normal pace with a relaxed expression.

So normal.

Like nothing's wrong.

Lila's shoulders shake as she reaches for a tissue on the table, her eyes filled with tears, and her makeup running everywhere. "Oh my God, this is so horrible. I need to go check on him." She starts to get up, but Ethan drapes an arm around her and pulls her back down. "Let Lyric do it, okay? You need to calm down before you talk to him." He looks at me for help.

I nod, getting to my feet. "Of course." I leave the living room and start up the stairs, but pause when I hear the two of them whispering.

"We knew this was a possibility when we took him in," Ethan says in a gentle tone. "We knew that those people were never caught, and that something might happen one day."

"But I never expected it to happen like this." Lila sniffles. "And did you see the look on his face. It was the same look he had when we picked him up that first day. God, what if he goes back to barely speaking." Tears flood her voice. "I just want him to be happy."

So do I. More than I want my own happiness.

I rush up the stairs and pause in front of Ayden's shut bedroom door, hesitating before I knock.

"Come in." His voice sounds so hollow that I almost start crying as hard as Lila. Instead, I collect myself and push the door open.

"Hey," I say as I tentatively enter.

He's lying on his stomach on the bed with a math text-book opened in front of him, doing his homework just like he said, as music thrums from the speakers of the stereo. He's grasping something in one of his hands.

He finishes writing out the problem before he glances up at me. "Did you need something?" he asks, the life in his grey eyes dead.

I press my lips together. "I just wanted to see if you were okay."

He shrugs, returning to his paper. "I'm fine. It's not like I didn't expect that to happen."

"You expected your brother to die?" I question as I close the door. "Why?"

He shrugs again, continuing to move the pencil across the paper. "I don't know. I just thought it could be a possi-bility after I found out he disappeared. I honestly am surprised any of us are alive, so ..."

I should just walk out. Give him time. The space he seems to want. But I can't leave him. So I sit down on the bed, highly aware when his grip on the pencil constricts.

"Ayden, talk to me." I suck in a breath before I dare place a hand on his back.

He goes as rigid as a board. "I don't know what to say." His voice cracks, and then he starts to cry, tears spilling out as he hunches over, hiding his face from me. "I don't think I can do this again—say goodbye." His hands free the object he was clutching, and a few tears slip from my eyes. It's a photo of him when he was younger, along with a young teenage boy and a girl. Probably his brother and sister.

All those years I spent wanting to experience life to the fullest, feel love and heartbreak, and now I feel so grateful that I haven't. Haven't been through what he has.

"Yes, you can." I rub his back as each of his sobs ruptures my heart. "I'm here for you. Whatever you need. I got your back."

But this time, it might not be so simple.

This time, I might not be able to help him.

Chapter 15

Ayden

Somehow in the midst of the chaos, I manage to fall asleep. When I wake up, my limbs are tangled with Lyric's, so much so that I can't tell where my arms start and her legs end.

Her head is nuzzled in the crook of my neck, her arm resting on my stomach, and her fingers are splayed across my rib cage where the tattoo is hidden beneath my shirt. The branded flesh scorches like it did the day it was put on me. The pain is one thing I've always been able to remember.

Charred skin.

The scent of dying flesh.

Listen closely.

You'll hear the scream.

Of someone breaking.

Burned alive from the inside.

I lie awake until the sunlight hits the window, watching Lyric sleep, trying to figure out how I managed to drift off with her in my bed.

I'd been such a mess last night, cold, distant, then I freaking lost it and cried in front of her. She'd held me, and instead of panicking, I'd felt better.

Felt safe.

Eventually, I leave the bed.

After slipping into the bathroom to change, I go downstairs, hoping no one else is awake. The moment I catch the scent of bacon, though, I know Lila is up and cooking.

I hesitate before I enter the kitchen, debating whether to run or stay. The obvious choice is to bolt. I used to do it all the time, and it was easy. Run away, live on the streets for a few days, then by the time I was found, the foster family didn't want me anymore. I have a feeling that things aren't going to be that uncomplicated with the Gregorys.

So, summoning a deep breath, I walk in.

Just as I guessed, Lila is standing near the stove, watching bacon sizzle from the pan. She's still in her pajamas, her hair unkempt, and her eyes have bags under them. She probably slept like crap last night, all because of me.

"Oh, hey," she says, startled when she sees me. "I

didn't know anyone was up. I was actually about to wake you."

"I just woke up." I rub at my wrists then trace the long, thin scars on the back of my hand. "I'm not sure how much trouble I'm going to be in, but you should probably know Lyric's asleep in my bed."

She reaches to turn the burner off. "Yeah, I know that. So do the Scotts. We thought it'd be okay for the night, considering." She moves the pan off to the side, then wipes her hands on a paper towel. "How about we have some breakfast and talk? There's a few things we need to discuss."

I stare at her with wariness as she crosses the kitchen to the table where there's a plate with eggs and a fork on it. She takes a seat then pats the chair next to her, and I reluctantly sit my ass down.

"How are you feeling?" she asks, inching the plate of eggs toward me.

I pick up the fork, but I don't feel very hungry. "Okay."

She tiredly sighs. "Ayden, I know you're not okay. You just lost your brother—you can't be okay."

"I lost him once before." I stab the fork into the eggs.

"Yeah, but this is different."

I stuff a bite of eggs into my mouth and slowly chew, killing time so I don't have to say anything. If I speak, I'm afraid I'll break again, like I did in front of Lyric last night.

"Ethan and I were talking last night, and we think you should start seeing the therapist a little more." She covers her hand over mine. "I know you've been doing well, but we just want to make sure you're okay." She pauses, and I know there's more. "There's something else. Something the cops mentioned when I walked them to the door."

I stop chewing. "What did they say?"

She squeezes my hand. "They think it could be beneficial if we tried some stuff to strike up your memories. They think it could help with the case if you could remember some of the details."

I clutch the fork so firmly the handle bends. "But how can they even know for sure that my brother's death had anything to do with the people who took us? It's been like, three years."

"They said there was some evidence that linked the two incidences together." She offers a sympathetic look. "I'm sure they'll be able to give us more information later on."

I inhale a large breath then exhale. "I don't want to talk about this anymore, if that's okay."

She moves her hand away from mine, nodding. "That's fine. We don't have to right now." She scoots the chair back from the table to stand up. "But, Ayden, I just want you to prepare yourself for, because it might be brought up the further they get into the case. Ethan and I will do everything we can to keep it as easy as possible on you, but some things might be out of our hands."

She returns to the bacon, leaving me with my eggs and my thoughts. There is a reason why I refuse to remember the week we spent in that home chained up. And while I can't actually recollect it, I know it has to be bad; otherwise, I wouldn't have suppressed the memories in the first place. But what if it could help with my brother's case?

After I finish my eggs, I head back upstairs. The house is still quiet when I slip back into my room, the only noise coming from the kitchen. I figure everyone is still asleep, so I'm surprised when I see Lyric sitting up on my bed, wide awake, the blankets tangled around her legs.

She's still wearing the shirt and jeans she had on yesterday, her blond hair surrounding her face, and she looks drained of all her sparkling energy.

"Hey." She sits up straighter as I shut the door. "Where did you go?"

"To eat some breakfast." I pause at the foot of the bed, staring at her. Through all the madness of last night, I haven't had time to think about what we did in the car. How we kissed. How I touched her. How I felt when she touched me back. I'm still so confused about it. So lost. About everything.

"Is everything okay?" She kicks the blankets off and scoots down the bed until she's kneeling on the mattress in front of me. "I don't want to push you," she starts, "but I need you to know that I'm here for you if you decide you need to talk."

"I don't feel like talking," I tell her then completely contradict myself seconds later as words pour out of my mouth. "They want me to try to remember stuff about three years ago."

"Who does?"

"The police. Lila... She didn't flat out say it, but I can tell she thinks I should. That it could help the case."

Her forehead creases as she combs her fingers through

her hair. "How does that even work? If you can't remember, then you can't remember, right?"

I shrug as I sink down onto the bed beside her. "There are ways. My therapist's mentioned a few before, but I always turned him down."

"What are you going to do?" She sketches a soothing path up and down my spine with her fingertip.

My instinctive shudder from her touch reminds me of what I face if I decide to do this. I want to, if nothing else, for my brother; but I'm also terrified out of my Goddamn mind.

"I don't know what I'm going to do."

"Well, I'm here for you, whatever you decide." She hugs her arms around me and pulls me closer to her.

I close my eyes, and for the briefest instant, try to allow my mind to remember. But as soon as my body begins to quiver, I give up. Instead, I lean into Lyric's touch, knowing that it's only a temporary fix, and that eventually I'm going to have to make a choice.

Face my future.

Or completely shut down.

Unraveling You

Jessica Sorensen

Unraveling You

About the Author

Jessica Sorensen is a *New York Times* and *USA Today* bestselling author that lives in the snowy mountains of Wyoming. When she's not writing, she spends her time reading and hanging out with her family.

Other books by Jessica Sorensen:

Unraveling You Series:

Unraveling You

Raveling You (Coming Jan. 2015)

The Coincidence Series:

The Coincidence of Callie and Kayden

The Redemption of Callie and Kayden

The Destiny of Violet and Luke

The Probability of Violet and Luke

The Certainty of Violet and Luke

The Resolution of Callie and Kayden

Unbeautiful (Coming Soon)

Seth & Grayson (Coming Soon)

The Secret Series:

The Prelude of Ella and Micha

The Secret of Ella and Micha

The Forever of Ella and Micha

The Temptation of Lila and Ethan

The Ever After of Ella and Micha

Lila and Ethan: Forever and Always

Ella and Micha: Infinitely and Always

The Shattered Promises Series:

Shattered Promises

Fractured Souls

Unbroken

Broken Visions

Scattered Ashes (Coming Soon)

Breaking Nova Series:

Breaking Nova

Saving Quinton

Delilah: The Making of Red

Nova and Quinton: No Regrets

Tristan: Finding Hope

Wreck Me

Ruin Me (Coming Soon)

The Fallen Star Series (YA):

The Fallen Star

The Underworld

The Vision

The Promise

The Fallen Souls Series (spin off from The Fallen Star):

The Lost Soul

The Evanescence

The Darkness Falls Series:

Darkness Falls

Darkness Breaks

Darkness Fades

The Death Collectors Series (NA and YA):

Ember X and Ember

Cinder X and Cinder

Spark X and Cinder (Coming Soon)

The Sins Series:

Seduction & Temptation

Sins & Secrets

Lies & Betrayal (Coming Soon)

Standalones

The Forgotten Girl

Unraveling You

<u>Coming Soon:</u>

Entranced

Steel & Bones

Connect with me online:

jessicasorensen.com

http://www.facebook.com/pages/Jessica-Sorensen/165335743524509

https://twitter.com/#!/jessFallenStar

CPSIA information can be obtained at www.ICGtesting.com
Printed in the USA
LVOW07s1115170915

454575LV00003B/86/P

9 781496 134271